VOW TO TREASURE

A FLYING CROSS RANCH ROMANCE 2

SHANAE JOHNSON

THOSE JOHNSON GIRLS

Edited by Alyssa Breck

First Edition January 2022

CHAPTER ONE

There was a *bump bump* as the plane came in for a landing. That was Joe Matthews's first indication that the road ahead of him would not be a smooth one. Whenever he was in the cockpit and he brought the craft back to earth, there was never a bump. Because Joe Matthews was precise, level-headed, and even-handed.

The swerve to the left, and then the hitch to the right as the pilot put on the brakes indicated that they were none of those things. Joe sat straight in his seat as many others braced themselves and tilted forward. During his time in the Air Force, he'd been in much hairier situations. Though it was his time in boardrooms and courtrooms negotiating and advising as a JAG officer that had been the most combat-laden.

As the commercial airliner slowed to taxi to the gate, a sense of calm came over Joe. Finally, he was back home. And home for good this time. His service in the Judge Advocate General Corp was finally done. What wasn't over was his need to serve. Though that need would be filled, as he took a different path on a different battlefield.

"Ladies and Gentlemen, the fasten your seat belts sign has been turned off, and it is now safe to move about the cabin. Thank you for flying with us today, and we wish you well on your next journey."

Joe stepped off the plane. It was a small puddle jumper aircraft that had flown him from the major airport in Yellowstone to his neck of the woods, which was still a ninety-minute car ride to his small hometown. So when he stepped off the plane, he stepped onto the tarmac and into fresh Montana air. With his lungs full, he looked up at the mountains, knowing he had a hard climb ahead as he prepared to step forward into his next journey in life.

Captain Joe Matthews was out of the war business. He was embarking on far more treacherous territory; the world of politics.

"There he is."

A smoke-filled, whiskey-laced voice broke through the soft rustle of wind of the day. That was the voice of Joe's campaign manager, soon to be chief of staff, Richard Wilson. The two men had gone to undergrad together. Where Joe finished his degree early and gone into the service, Rich had taken a more scenic route on his path through education and had finally graduated three years ago with a handful of half majors and a bucketful of minors that were cobbled together into a completed B.S.

Rich could've graduated at any time with parents that paid an endowment to the school. He just enjoyed campus life too much. Aside from the degree, Rich had collected people. He knew everyone that was worthy of knowing in the state of Montana.

"Ladies and Gentlemen, Cowboys and Ranch hands, may I present to you the next United States Attorney for the great state of Montana."

Rich spread his arms wide and made a sound at the back of his throat meant to mimic a roaring crowd. His antics were met with a couple of stares, some eye rolls, but mostly huffs of annoyance as passengers tried to wheel their way around the two men stopped in the middle of the tarmac.

"I don't think they share your enthusiasm, Rich," said Joe as he retrieved his bag from the plane-side cart.

"That's just because they don't know this golden boy yet." Rich clapped him on the shoulder as they headed into the terminal. "They'll learn you're a hometown boy who done good. An underdog from foster care who rose through the ranks of the military to become a top JAG officer. Man, they'd eat this stuff up if we took it to Hollywood. Which reminds me, we have a meeting with a producer at the end of the month."

At some point, they'd picked up their pace. Joe only realized that because he was trying to catch his breath. He was still in top form, but Rich could be a whirlwind that would eat up lesser men and women and spit them out whole with his big dreams. The man talked a big game. Joe had realized over the past year that his old college bum of a friend could deliver.

"You have a lot of meetings this week," Rich continued, pulling out a handheld device that looked like it could launch missiles. "We're going to have a party announcing your interest in just a few days. All of the council members will be in attendance. Then I've got community events scheduled and—"

"Rich, I just got back. I'd like to at least go home and see my dad."

"Yeah, sure, sure. Which reminds me, we need to get a photo op with you and the old man. A preacher father? That is going to do great with the religious demographics."

Joe didn't even bother to sigh out loud. This was Rich. Everything was staged with him and used to an advantage.

Joe wouldn't let that happen to his father. Haran Matthews had had a heart attack not too long ago. The man needed rest. Joe still felt guilty that he and his brothers hadn't been here for their father in his time of need. The man had been there for each of them at all the important parts in their lives. Seeing his dad was priority number one.

"Commissioner Benson is available for dinner tomorrow night. He's the one that's still on the fence about you as acting D.A."

The last District Attorney had retired suddenly because of health reasons. The board of commissioners had the right to appoint an acting D.A. in her absence. With his credentials, Joe was the top candidate for the post.

"Like most of the commissioners, Benson is very traditional," Rich went on. "He doesn't trust a man that isn't leg-shackled. I have the perfect woman for you for that. I've set that up for later this afternoon."

Now Joe did sigh out loud. He hadn't been on board with this idea of a fake fiancée the first time Rich had brought it up. Joe wasn't good at faking anything. Most soldiers weren't unless it came to pain tolerance and torture. Faking a relationship certainly sounded like torture. Especially when his heart had decided long ago that it belonged to one woman.

"You'll like Charlotte," Rich was saying. "She's a lawyer, like you. Not military, but she's definitely active. Man, wait till you see the legs on her."

"Rich, I'm not going to pretend I'm in love with a woman to get a job."

"Who said anything about love? It's a business arrangement. Isn't that what marriage is?"

Not for Joe. For years he'd tried to convince his heart that it was illogical to pine for Foxy James. She was the most impractical, irrational, incongruous, beautiful, bold, bright—

Joe gave his head a shake. He'd entirely lost his train of thought. What were they talking about?

"She's exactly the type of woman a District Attorney would have as a wife," Rich was saying.

Those words brought Joe back to reality. Foxy James—even her name—was not political wife material. Foxy was a mess of curly hair that never behaved. Her skirts were too short. She also had a penchant for wearing sparkly colored sneakers that mismatched those short skirts. And then there was the other matter… she believed she was psychic.

"If you want to achieve your goal of someday soon becoming the US Attorney for this state, then the least you can do is meet her for lunch later today."

Meet her? Not Foxy. The woman who was a perfect political wife. The woman who would help Joe achieve his goal of serving at a higher office where he could help keep the scales of justice balanced.

That was his chosen purpose in life. That was his dream. That's what would be his legacy after a rough start in life, where the scales were tipped out of his favor. He'd achieved balance, and he wanted to do that for others. With the right partner, one who was his equal, he could make that dream come true.

"Joe!"

Joe looked up at the sound of that familiar voice. His grin split wide as he saw his brother. Charlie's and Joe's smiles matched, as did their hazel eyes. Charlie held out his tanned hand. Joe clasped his brother's hand with his brown one. Then the two embraced, squeezing tight and clapping each other on the back.

It had been far too long since he'd seen his foster brother. Sure, he was surrounded by brothers in the military, but there was nothing like being in the presence of the man he'd grown up with.

Charlie and Joe and the other four Matthews boys had been through a different kind of trenches together. They'd come up through the foster care system and survived. There should be a medal for fighting on those battlegrounds. But the six boys from Bright Horizons had been rewarded with something far greater; a father in the form of Haran Matthews.

"It's good to see you, man." Joe gave Charlie another squeeze before letting him go.

Charlie smelled like home. Like hay, homecoming, and horses. Joe had a sudden itch to be back on the ranch. To be back in open fields. To mount a horse and race through the valley. To hear his father's laugh and see the sparkle in the old man's eyes.

"Good to see you again, Rich," said Charlie.

"You, too," said Rich. "Just remember, we have shared custody of your brother now. I need him back by lunchtime."

Charlie snorted, but he didn't disagree. Though Joe and Rich had been tight during college, no one could compete with the bond the brothers shared.

"You ready to go?" Charlie asked Joe. "Savy's double-parked outside."

"Sav's here?"

"Yeah, she couldn't wait to see you."

"So, it's just the two of you?" Joe asked, hoping no one could hear the eagerness in his voice.

"Yeah, it's a hike out here. We kinda used the car ride as a date night. We don't get much with the kids at home."

Joe nodded, his mind not on his brother's words. Instead, he was trying to think of another way to ask where Foxy was. No one knew about his heart's long-ago decision that Foxy was the one for him. He'd kept it from his brothers and from Foxy herself.

Foxy had told him as a kid that she'd had a premonition about her one true love. As soon as she'd said those three words, *one true love*, Joe had known she was his. Even when Foxy insisted she wouldn't meet her mystery man until she was older.

"So, Tricksy's at the ranch with the kids?" asked Joe.

"No, Tricks is still on the road." Charlie hefted one of Joe's bags over his shoulder and began walking toward the exit doors to Ground Transportation.

It took Joe a moment to get his feet to move. There was still no mention of Foxy.

"Who's minding the kids?" Joe tried again.

"Dad is," said Charlie.

Finally, Joe just gave up and came out with it. "And Foxy?"

"Ummm," Charlie thought about it for a moment. The silence stretched on so long that Joe thought he might've forgotten the question. "I think she went to town to see Travis Ramos."

Joe's heart skipped a beat. Not the upbeat skip of a man in love. The thunk down into the stomach of a man who'd been gut-punched.

The love of his life was dating someone. She was older now. It was the future. Travis might be her dream man. He might not. The fact of the case was that Foxy hadn't seen Joe in that vision. Even if she saw him now, he still wouldn't be the man of her dreams. So what was he waiting for?

Before he stepped out of the airport, Joe turned to Rich and said, "I'll see you and your friend at lunch."

CHAPTER TWO

"Travis, why won't you give me a reference?"

"You mean to tell me that as a psychic, you don't know?"

Foxy bit her tongue, trying to hold back the familiar retort. Why was that always the taunt everyone threw at her? *Didn't you know I was coming? Didn't you know the answers to the test you just epically failed? Didn't you know that guy, or girl, was a scumbag before you befriended them?*

No, she didn't know those things because she was not a psychic. Foxy hated the term psychic. It was such a catchall for anyone who had a heightened sense of awareness like her.

That heightened sense could come in many

forms. Some people heard things in their minds. Kinda like Yoda and other Jedi masters using the Force to communicate or put suggestions in weaker minds. Though the sense of clairaudience was typically one-sided.

Others who were gifted might see images and scenes play out in their mind's eye. This clairvoyance might be in the form of metaphorical symbols. Sometimes they might see a flash of actual events from the past. Sometimes they might foresee a hazy possibility of the future.

Foxy wasn't afflicted with that ability either, and she was thankful for it. Her day-to-day life rivaled that of what could be seen on movie screens most days with an irresponsible mother who had dragged her daughters out on the road, into back-alley dives and smoke-filled bars where they saw all manner of things no adolescent should've witnessed.

Foxy was also thankful that she wasn't claircognizant. She didn't experience the feelings of others. Living in a house full of troubled youth both as a child and now as an adult, she would've never gotten to sleep buried under the weight of their feelings, much less her own. It was the thought of the children currently in her care that made her humble herself and try again with her former boss.

"I'm not psychic," she explained patiently. "What I am is clairsentient. It means the messages come through to me as a strong feeling. Like a gut reaction."

"Hmm," said Travis as he rang up the order of a departing lunch party. "And your gut didn't tell you that you were the worst waitress in the history of this restaurant?"

"Was not," was Foxy's professional retort.

Travis closed the cash register with a smack of his palm that made the machine ding. "You argued with people over what they chose to order off the menu."

"I didn't need my abilities to tell me that Mr. Jensen was one more steak away from a heart attack."

Mr. Jensen had barely fit into the booth. His breath had been short as he'd battled with the furniture over the effort. Once uncomfortably inside the booth, his belly had pushed so far up on the table that he could've balanced his glass of soda on it. He alternately reached for his cup of sparkling sugar and scratched at his jaw and chest, clear signs that a heart attack could be imminent. It hadn't been her gut. It had been her own eyes that had told Foxy that one more sip, or one more bite of rich food, could be his last.

Foxy had been wrong. It had been ten more steaks before Mr. Jensen landed himself in the hospital. And even after his bypass, she'd seen him sneaking into the fast-food joint in the next town.

"Then we developed those long waits because you started doing readings for dining customers," Travis was going on as he wiped down the plastic-covered menus, giving the grime more attention than he did her.

"I don't do readings because I'm not a psychic," Foxy corrected. "What I did was tell my neighbors who came into this fine establishment what my gut told me about them. It would be irresponsible of me not to."

Travis slapped the semi-clean menu down on the counter. "That wasn't your job. Your job was to take their orders and serve them with a smile. You weren't capable of that."

"I did smile at—"

"And now you want a job being a psychic for troubled youth?"

Foxy opened her mouth to tell him once again that she wasn't a psychic. It was a moot point. So, she shut her mouth and breathed in through her nose, trying to tap into the calm in her gut that told her that getting a letter of recommendation from Travis was a sure thing.

Clearly, she'd gotten this one wrong, too. That was the thing about being gifted with heightened senses. She was aware enough to get the message. But she didn't always interpret the meaning correctly.

Foxy often got the feeling that someone was about to call or come over. The phone might ring that moment or an hour later. They might show up on her doorstep later that day or next week. The feelings didn't come with a date-time stamp. But they always came true… eventually.

Now clearly wasn't the time when Travis would give her a glowing review. The problem was, she needed that letter of recommendation sooner rather than later if she was going to complete her application as an Elevated Care Foster Parent. She had kids counting on her, one in particular.

With that sense of urgency, Foxy turned on her heel and left the restaurant. Working here at Ramos's Deli and Cafe hadn't been her only job. She'd had other odd jobs in the town since she'd left the stage behind.

She and her two sisters had once toured the

country as a singing trio, even after their mother had passed away from an overdose. But singing hadn't been Foxy's passion. People were. Especially younger people.

Like her older sister, Savy, Foxy had chosen to dedicate her life to helping troubled youth in the foster system. Kids with no responsible parents, or available guardians, or no family at all. But Foxy wanted to help on a higher level.

Too many of the kids in foster homes suffered from trauma and emotional shock. They often had long-lasting psychological effects that traditional foster parents couldn't manage. Having been there and done that, Foxy could help. Foxy wanted to help.

She'd completed the pre-service training. She'd passed the Fingerprint Criminal Record check, to many others' surprise. Now all she needed to complete the approval process was to gain two letters of reference. Surprisingly, this was proving the trickiest part.

She only had one letter so far. From Father Matthews. She needed one more. But she didn't bother trying to contact any of the old bar, club, or stage managers, thinking they wouldn't be the best judges of character.

The Danillos remembered her at the pizza parlor. But they wouldn't give her a recommendation since she'd only worked there for three weeks as a teenager. And she'd left without notice when her mom had snagged her and her sisters for a two-month gig on the road.

Being the youngest of the James sisters, Foxy hadn't stayed in high school long enough for the teachers to get a feel for her. Ms. Wright, her chorus teacher, remembered her. But what she remembered most was Foxy mentioning she had a feeling that Ms. Wright and Mr. Gerken, the football coach, would get together.

Foxy had been right. Sort of. They'd gotten married. Had a child. And then the football coach up and left the chorus teacher for the home economics teacher. It had been one of the biggest scandals in Honor Valley history.

Technically, Foxy had been right. Just not right enough to warrant a glowing recommendation from the first Mrs. Gerken. Foxy was running out of options.

Lifting her head to the wind, Foxy waited for a feeling to tell her which way to go. The wind picked up to her right, and she turned to put the air at her back. There had to be someone in this town who would vouch for her.

And then she saw it. A sign in the sky. Charlotte O'Dell, Family Law Practice. Ms. O'Dell had gotten Foxy out of a jam once. She only hoped the lawyer could do so again.

CHAPTER THREE

There was nothing like the smell of home. The Flying Cross Ranch smelled of fresh-cut grass, of turned earth laced with manure. Joe's nostrils flared as he took in the familiar scent. He opened his mouth so that he could gulp down lungfuls of the stuff. It was the smell of belonging, the scent of security, the knowledge that he was safe in this place.

In his younger years, his sense of smell had been his first defense. Clean smells were far and few between. Joe had spent the first part of his life sleeping on lumpy mattresses that had sometimes been used as toilets. He'd hid in corners that smelled of rotted food. He'd cowered in closets of unwashed clothes.

Joe knew he was made out of love. The letter from his dead mother told him so. He could only just barely remember her face. Her blonde curls and blue eyes with pink lips that stretched into a smile so bright that it threatened to overtake the single memory he had of her.

His mother, Janie, had told him that she loved him and that his father had too. The father that Joe had never met because he'd been lost to an IED in Afghanistan. Sergeant DeSean Curtis had never met his only son because Janie Horton's parents hadn't liked the look of the tall, dark man covered in tattoos.

And so when Janie returned home after DeSean's burial, they'd pushed their daughter to give up the little brown baby for adoption. When she refused, they cut her off for three years... until she passed away in a factory accident. It was when Joe was deposited on his grandparents' doorstep that he first learned to hide. By the time he was tossed into foster care, he'd gotten good at the survival tactic.

Joe had stopped hiding when he'd come to the home of Haran and Tessa Matthews. Every room smelled of wide-open spaces and blooming flowers. The beds were soft and warm. The clothes were always washed and folded in the closets. The bathrooms spotless and odorless, even after one of his brothers finished their business inside. The Flying Cross Ranch was the sweetest smelling and safest place on the earth.

The sky over the ranch house was a little dimmer with the absence of his adoptive mother. Joe had taken Tessa Matthews's death as hard as he had his mother's. It was the love of his adoptive father that kept him strong.

Haran Matthews smiled down at him from the porch. The clouds parted at that second, sending two rays of sunshine down as the two men embraced. Joe was certain that it was his two heavenly mothers shining down their love.

Joe's adoptive father had hugged him as soon as he came in the door to the ranch house. When Father Matthews moved to let his son go, Joe squeezed tighter, needing to hold on just a few moments longer to inhale his scent. He'd nearly lost the man that had saved his life to an overworked heart. And so, Joe held on a little longer.

When he finally released his father was when he saw a ragtag group of kids looking suspiciously at him. The look was reminiscent of anytime strangers came to the ranch when he and his brothers were young. For months, likely even years, the Matthews boys feared someone coming to Flying Cross to take them from their adoptive parents.

"Children, I'd like you to meet my son," said Father Matthews. "Joe, this is Denny."

The tallest kid nodded his head upward, his shrewd eyes a challenge as he eyed Joe. That was the leader of this bunch.

"This little princess is LaTisha."

A brown-skinned girl with braids bit at the inside of her lip as she regarded Joe. Where Denny might be the leader, this one looked like the brains of the bunch.

"This one here is Miguel."

Miguel was the only one of the group that offered Joe a smile and a wave. The dark-haired kid looked Joe up and down, but not as though he was sizing up whether or not he could take him. Miguel regarded Joe as though he were trying to determine what gift to bring him for his birthday.

"I'm making enchiladas for dinner," said Miguel. "Some with chicken and others with only fish because Tisha has decided she's a vegetarian."

"Fish isn't a vegetable," said LaTisha, her eyes rolled skyward as though this wasn't the first time she'd stated that fact.

Father Matthews smiled in his good-natured

way at the two before turning to the last kid in the bunch. "The last kid here is Ashton, who prefers to be called Ashtray."

Ashtray's blond hair was done in neat little corn-rows. He wore a Wu Tang T-shirt and jeans that sagged low on his skinny body. "Yo, you spit any lyrics, bro?"

Joe bit back the retort that was on the tip of his tongue. This was just a kid. Still, this kid needed to learn some respect.

"You can call me Captain Joe, Ash… tray." Joe figured if he was going to ask the kid for some respect in how to address him, he'd have to show respect as well. "And I'm not a lyricist. I'm a lawyer."

A tendril of fear shot through the kids' eyes. They all took a step back and closer to Father Matthews. Even Denny, the fearless leader, looked piqued around the eyes.

"Relax," said Joe. "I'm not here to take any of you away. This is my home, too. I used to be a foster kid until Father Matthews adopted me."

"Ms. Savy and Mr. Charlie are going to adopt us," said Miguel.

"I know," said Joe. "I'm helping them with that paperwork."

That statement broke the tension in the crowd.

But there was still a wary unease. Joe understood the sentiment. He was the new guy to them. It always took foster kids a while to trust adults.

"Why don't you go and get settled, son. I had Savy make up the guest room."

"Oh, um, I was going to stay in the guest house."

"Savy and Foxy are staying in the guest house."

"Oh? Well, I thought, since Savy and Charlie are getting married, that…"

"That what?"

Joe couldn't meet his father's gaze. If he dared, he knew the man would see right through his intentions. But what exactly were Joe's intentions toward Foxy?

"This is still a Christian household," his father was saying. "Savy and Charlie can sleep in the same room after they take their vows."

The children giggled but were quieted after a stern look from Father Matthews. When that stern look came back to Joe, the grown man squirmed in his shoes.

"Although you and Foxy are like brother and sister…" Father Matthews waited a couple beats before finishing his thoughts. "It would be improper for a man in your position to be bunking with a single woman."

For long moments after, Joe thought on that pause his father had taken. Did Father Matthews know about his childhood feelings for Foxy? Were they still just childhood feelings? Joe had already established that Foxy couldn't be the woman of his dreams, not if who she was was antithetical to him achieving his dreams.

In the kitchen, Joe opened the fridge to grab a cold drink. As the cold air sailed out of the icebox, so did the scent of strawberries. The sweet and tart scent sent Joe back into a time that had felt like a dream.

There had been strawberries on her breath. There always was. Either from the lip balm she applied or the fruit itself. It was her favorite.

Joe had never cared for the fruit. The seeds always got stuck in his teeth. He'd avoid them at the dining table until that day. That day, when Foxy James had looked up at him and pressed her berry-glossed lips against his.

He had always been a practical child, not prone to emotional outbursts. He hadn't cried when his mother died. He hadn't cried when his grandparents abandoned him. The one and only time Joe Matthews had cried was the day Foxy James had kissed him because the moment her sweet, berry lips met his, a single tear slipped down his cheek to turn the kiss bitter.

Foxy had taught Joe about soulmates. He'd thought that she was his. But she'd never said that he was hers. Logically, if she didn't see him that way, then she couldn't be his soulmate. Someone else must be.

Or maybe there were no such things as soulmates at all.

What Joe did know was that his sole purpose for being on this earth was to keep the scales of justice in balance. He could do a lot of good in this world with a bit more power in his hands. Becoming the District Attorney would afford him some of that power. Dating a woman like Rich had suggested—what was her name again? Charlotte?—could give him a stronghold.

With that thought, Joe closed the refrigerator door, shutting out the scent of tart berries.

CHAPTER FOUR

Foxy rolled the gloss onto her lips. The sweet taste of strawberries touched the tip of her tongue as she did so. The fruity taste instantly settled her, bringing her racing mind back to the simple pleasures of childhood.

The James sisters had grown up so poor that candy was an unattainable dream. Fruit from the fields was their only treat. When strawberries were in season during the summer months, Foxy would run through the fields and gorge, feeling like she was the richest kid on earth.

She had her hands out now as she stood at the door to Charlotte O'Dell's offices. Foxy pressed her top and bottom lip together, smoothing out the gloss. This was her last shot at not only making her dream come true but of helping children in need.

That's what Ms. O'Dell did. She helped kids in need. She wouldn't say no. She couldn't say no.

Throwing her shoulders back, lifting her chin, and stretching her mouth into a wide, friendly grin, Foxy entered the offices of Charlotte O'Dell, Family Law Practice. Sitting in the center of the white-walled reception room was Foxy's first obstacle.

"Do you have an appointment?" asked the secretary. Her dark hair was pulled back into a severe bun. The glasses sitting on the tip of her nose had lenses too thin to be prescriptive.

"No, but I am a former client of Ms. O'Dell," Foxy said as she skirted around the secretary's desk. "I just have a quick question to ask her."

The woman might be small, but she was quick. She shot out of her chair and was around the desk, blocking Foxy's way in an instant. "I'm sorry, but Ms. O'Dell is on her way to lunch."

"I just have a quick question about some paperwork."

Foxy feinted right, but unfortunately, the other woman predicted her move and threw out her spindly arms to block Foxy. Foxy heard the taunt in her head; *Didn't you see that one coming, little Miss Psychic?*

"I can schedule you for next week," the secretary said through clenched teeth.

Foxy put on her most winning smile and tried diplomacy again. "Really, what I have to say won't take more than—"

"Foxy James? Is that you?"

A pretty blonde poked her head out of the office door. Charlotte O'Dell was forever put together. She wore a deep purple business suit that belted just under her breastbone, accentuating her small waist. Her lips were a muted pink, but there wasn't a smell coming off her mouth like Foxy's berry gloss. That's because it was likely actual lipstick from a fancy department counter or retail cosmetics store and not gloss bought from the corner convenience store.

"What is it this time?" Charlotte asked as she slipped a scarf around her shoulders, which perfectly matched her pulled-together outfit. "Did you attempt to ride another man like a horse?"

The secretary dropped her arms and stepped back. She looked up at Foxy with interest now. Foxy took in a deep breath and let it out.

"It's not what you think," said Foxy.

Charlotte chuckled. Though she was a woman,

no one would ever accuse the serious lawyer of giggling. Charlotte's voice was smokey, like Foxy's oldest sister Savy. "I represented Ms. James a year ago when she was charged with assault."

"It wasn't assault," Foxy explained. "It was self-defense."

Charlotte raised a perfectly plucked eyebrow.

"It was," insisted Foxy. "Just not for myself. For the horse."

The secretary turned from Foxy and looked at her boss for clarification. That rankled Foxy. It was her story, after all. She was the one with the first-hand account.

"Ms. James accused Auggie Fenton of animal abuse. Which is what any animal-loving citizen should do if they witness such a thing. Only Ms. James had never met Mr. Fenton."

The secretary turned to regard Foxy again. When Foxy opened her mouth to explain herself, the woman turned back to Charlotte for the facts of Foxy's story.

"The police went on to question Mr. Fenton. Only to learn that he didn't own any pets. When the police returned to question her, Ms. James said she'd had a feeling that Mr. Fenton was abusing animals. She's a psychic, you see."

Now the secretary scrunched up her nose as she peered at Foxy. Foxy peered back, certain now that those thin lenses held no prescription.

"I'm clairsentient," Foxy corrected the record. "It means I get feelings."

Foxy couldn't tell if the secretary was now looking at her with interest or scorn. Charlotte was grinning with amusement that was uncommon for the serious lawyer. Foxy supposed her case had been one for the books.

"Turns out she was right," Charlotte continued. "Mr. Fenton had horse manes in the trunk of his car. He'd been going to ranches and cutting off horse manes for weeks and selling them on the black market for hair weaves and extensions."

The secretary subconsciously touched her tightly wound bun. On second glance, her mane looked far too thick and lush to be all her own hair. She likely was a customer of store-bought tresses.

"It's an awful crime," said Foxy. "Horses use their tails to communicate, for warmth, and pest control. Imagine someone coming and hacking off your limb. It takes them a year to grow back."

"Mr. Fenton only got away with a misdemeanor," said Charlotte. "That still chafes."

Even though Charlotte O'Dell was a bit of a stiff,

with little imagination, and often took things liter-
ally, Foxy had liked her lawyer. Charlotte was laser-
focused when it came to the scales of justice. That
trait reminded Foxy of her childhood best friend,
Joe Matthews.

Even as a little boy, Joe had been a serious man.
He'd trail behind Foxy as the voice of conscience on
her right shoulder. Foxy had never been interested
in breaking the law. She did have a habit of telling
people about the feelings she got that involved them.
That got her in a stitch or two. Joe was always there,
bailing her out with his calm logic.

Joe was due back to the ranch soon. Foxy
couldn't wait to see her old friend. She should intro-
duce him to Charlotte. The two would be a perfect
match. That is, if Charlotte would help her.

"What can I do for you, Ms. James?"

"I was hoping to get a letter of recommendation
from you."

"Recommendation? For what?"

"I want to be an Elevated Care Foster Parent."

Charlotte tilted her head like a bird. The move-
ment again reminded her of Joe Matthews. Joe
would often gaze at Foxy in the same way, as if she
were some creature that he didn't understand. A
creature that might open its hand with a treat or

turn a trick where she'd pounce on him and swallow him whole.

"All right," said Charlotte.

"All right?" asked Foxy.

"I'll do it."

"You will?"

"Give me until the end of the day. I have a lunch date in just—" Charlotte looked up and smiled. It was a smile of someone who saw a tall drink of water coming toward them on a hot desert day. "I think that's him arriving."

A sensation came over Foxy. One that told her something important was about to happen. Whoever this guy was that was coming for Charlotte, he was soulmate material. Foxy could feel it in her gut.

It was the warm sensation, like the brush of the ocean against the tip of her toes on a sandy beach. Like the snuggle under the covers after the sheets came out of the dryer. Like the security she felt anytime Father Matthews gave her a hug and a smile.

Foxy turned around, eager to witness the first awareness of true love unfolding in real life. She was met with a familiar face. A face from her childhood that had aged into the sharp angles and strong lines of a fully grown man. A fully grown man with a muscled chest that pushed against his collared shirt and filled out his long slacks.

When Joe Matthews's gaze found Foxy's, his head tilted to the side in the same birdlike motion of his youth. Treat or trick, it seemed to ask. Foxy didn't give him a moment to make up his mind. She launched herself into her friend's arms and let herself drown in the warm ocean feel of him, the just-dried sheets of him, the same secure hug that his father was famous for giving to those he loved and cherished.

Joe Matthews, her best friend from childhood, was home.

CHAPTER FIVE

"That's her."

Never had a truth rang so loudly in any man's ears. Those were the words that played in his ears over the last hour as Joe tried to convince himself that Foxy was not the one for him. That this childhood infatuation with her was long over. That there had to be someone else out there, a far more appropriate woman that he was meant to spend his life with.

The moment that he walked into the doors of Charlotte O'Dell's law offices, the first thing he saw was Foxy's dark, springy curls. The second thing he saw were her bright, expressive eyes. The last thing he saw was her brilliant sunshine of a smile.

"That's her."

The words were spoken out loud, but they hadn't come from Joe's mouth. They were from Rich, who walked into the offices beside Joe. So, he saw it too? He saw that Foxy was the only woman for him? Joe now had no reason to ever doubt or question his friend again.

And it looked like Foxy finally saw it too.

Her entire face lit up like a Christmas tree when she turned and saw him. The springy curls atop her head bounced as though they danced to a spirited jig as she clapped her hands together and bounced up and down in delight. With each step she took toward him, her grin spread wider, lighting him up from the outside in and then from the inside out.

Foxy spread her arms like a new bird taking its first flight. There was no fear of falling. No thought of failure. Because Joe was there to catch her as she flung herself into his wide-open arms.

Joe was forever catching her. Foxy had a habit of not looking before she leaped. Of speaking before she thought through her words. Of taking action before making a solid plan

As kids, Joe had always trailed behind Foxy. He never told her not to go and do something crazy because then he wouldn't have a reason to catch her.

And Joe was always waiting for any opportunity to catch her.

He caught her now. He wrapped his arms around her lush form. His fingers interlaced and locked the moment she was inside his embrace.

His nose went into her hair. The curls tickled him, bunching around him and welcoming him home.

He inhaled the sweet scent of strawberries, and his stomach grumbled, reminding him he hadn't eaten since he'd landed. In fact, he couldn't remember the last time his belly had been filled. Suddenly, Joe was starving. He had never wanted anything more in his life than he wanted the woman in his arms.

The woman of his dreams tilted her head up and looked at him. With her grin firmly in place, Foxy said his name. "Joe."

It was a sigh. It was a homecoming. It was the answer to a prayer.

Joe was transported back all those years ago to the time when he'd tasted her lips. It had been a dark moment, the darkest of his life. The day that she had been taken from him. Just as his mother had. Just as his father had.

Only it was different with Foxy. Because Foxy

still walked this earth. But he couldn't walk beside her. He couldn't catch her if she stumbled. He wouldn't be there if she fell.

All that was over. Because she was here now, and he would never let her go again.

Joe had Foxy in his arms. And now she saw it. Everybody saw it. They belonged together.

A throat cleared behind him. Joe ignored the intrusion. He was far busier, calculating if he could kiss her now or if he should wait until later.

"I didn't realize how much I missed you until just now," said Foxy.

"I've missed you every day since the last time I saw you," Joe said, thrilled that he could finally speak his truth out loud. "Three thousand five hundred and sixty-seven days."

Foxy threw her head back and laughed. Joe still held her tightly. Had he not, she may have toppled backward. He would've never let that happen. In fact, he locked his arms tighter around her. How had the woman survived without him?

"Do you hear that, Ms. O'Dell?" Foxy said over her shoulder. "Joe is excellent at math. Whenever I had an algebra problem, I went to him."

O'Dell? Why was that name familiar? For the first time since he'd come into the building, Joe cast a glance at the other woman in the room. Tall, blonde, dressed in a power suit that was tailored to highlight her slim assets.

"He's smart," Foxy continued. "And handsome."

The woman, Ms. O'Dell, lifted an eyebrow and nodded. Again, a throat cleared behind Joe. All of his attention was on Foxy. Foxy made a move to step back, out of his embrace. Joe held tight, reluctant to let her go.

"I thought we weren't expecting you until later," said Foxy.

"What?" said Joe. "Don't tell me you didn't see me coming."

"As a matter of fact, I did see you. We were just talking about you." Again, Foxy motioned behind her to the blonde woman. "Wasn't I just telling you about him, Ms. O'Dell?"

"You were, indeed." Ms. O'Dell extended her hand. "Hello, Captain Matthews. It's nice to finally meet you."

Why did that name sound familiar? Joe didn't have time to remember. With his attention diverted to Ms. O'Dell, Foxy was pulling out of his hold. Joe supposed he should let her go. They would have time to embrace when they were alone. Besides, he was being rude to her friend.

Joe took the hand offered him by Foxy's friend. "Please, call me Joe. Any friend of Foxy's is a friend of mine."

"I was hoping you and Charlotte would become good friends," said Rich from behind him.

Joe had entirely forgotten the man was even there. He'd hardly noticed anyone else the moment he'd seen Foxy. Only just now, he realized there was a third woman in the room. She sat behind a desk, watching the small group with rapt attention.

"Joe," Rich spoke slowly, as though Joe were a slow learner, "this is Charlotte O'Dell. The one I was telling you about."

The one? What one? Foxy was the one.

If possible, Foxy's face lit up even brighter as she looked from Joe to Charlotte. "Is Joe your lunch date?" Foxy asked her friend. "I knew it. Didn't I tell you you two should meet? And now you are."

Joe had barely glanced at Charlotte, but now he took a good hard look at her. As he did, his entire reason for coming into town came back to him. He was here to meet Charlotte O'Dell, a woman Rich thought would be perfect for him to date in an effort to win over the very conservative Board of Commissioners in charge of appointing the next District Attorney.

"I have such a good feeling about this." Foxy reached down and grabbed Joe's hand. Then she reached out and took Charlotte's hand. She raised them both to her chest as though she were blessing the two of them.

Joe's brain was still trying to catch up. Foxy hadn't been the one that Rich had brought him to meet. It was Charlotte. Not only did Rich think that Joe and Charlotte were a perfect match, apparently, so did Foxy.

"Don't let me interrupt fate." Foxy lowered both of Joe's and Charlotte's hands and joined them together. Once Foxy clasped their hands together, she stepped back and gave Joe a wink. "You can tell me all about your date when you get home tonight."

And with that, Foxy walked backward toward the exit. She didn't look where she was going. She didn't watch her step. Miraculously, she didn't trip, or stumble, or fall.

At least this time, Joe hadn't been left with a mess to clean up. Instead, he was left holding another woman's hand while the woman his heart beat for didn't cast a single glance backward.

CHAPTER SIX

There was a pep to Foxy's step as she left the law offices of Charlotte O'Dell, Family Law Practice. The sun was no higher in the sky, but the day felt brighter. That's because Foxy loved when she got to witness one of her feelings come to light. And Joe Matthews had always been a bright light.

When they were kids, he'd balked at the notion of a soul mate. He'd demanded that Foxy prove her theory of one true love with facts and figures. She could only offer him her feelings on the matter.

That chemical reaction that only she could experience inside her own body did not suffice for Joe. Yet, still, he remained her shadow while they were kids. Always at her back or by her side when her gut feelings got her into scrapes. And now, today, Joe had come face to face with the mate to his soul. He would finally know what she meant when she told him of those feelings of light and warmth and happiness.

A shadow crossed over Foxy from above. She knew it for what it was; jealousy. For years, Foxy had watched as a spectator looking from the inside out as she got the feeling that two people were meant to be together. She watched them meet. Watched the recognition dawn that they were in the presence of something big. Watch them fall in love and begin their happily ever after. Or sometimes, their happy for now.

All the while, she waited for her dream man. Where was he? He was running super late. That's where he was.

More than anything in the world, Foxy wanted a man that she could lean on when life got hard. She wanted arms to fold around her and keep her warm. She wanted a strong heartbeat to pound against her cheek while holding her close. She wanted the security that came with knowing that she'd found her person, the one who would stick by her through thick and thin and never let her down.

Joe had once filled that role when they were kids.

Even though he thought most of her schemes and actions harebrained, he'd always watched over her and was there when things didn't go as planned. And if she remembered correctly, even as a scrawny kid, Joe Matthews had given the best hugs.

Maybe Foxy could sneak in a few more of those hugs from Joe while she waited impatiently for her soulmate to show up? Though that would have to depend on Charlotte. The family law legalese didn't seem like the jealous type. Though Charlotte's eyebrow had raised when Joe held Foxy a little too long.

Charlotte didn't have anything to worry about. She and Joe had been childhood friends. There wasn't anything between them except fond memories and a few heart-pounding moments that were typical in foster care.

While their older siblings Charlie and Savy had had an epic love affair, Joe and Foxy had never so much as held hands or shared a chaste kiss. And why would they? They were only friends.

Charlotte O'Dell was a lucky woman. The universe had matched her to a great guy. Foxy just hoped the powers that be would finally get around to plopping her soulmate on her doorstep.

Turning the key in the foster care van, the old

bag of gears coughed and sputtered. With a second turn of the key, the engine turned over. She and her sister were supposed to take the vehicle in for a tune-up. They hadn't had the time with the move from the foster house to the ranch. Foxy hadn't had any premonitions of the van breaking down, so she decided to put it off another day.

The van carried her safely back to the Flying Cross Ranch. When she put it in park, it gave a satisfied shudder, as though it knew it would be idle for the rest of the day. The van was the only thing on this ranch that would be idle for the time being. Chores were in full swing on the land.

Savy, Miguel, and LaTisha were in the garden. From this distance, Foxy couldn't tell if they were weeding, seeding, or tossing a salad. Whatever they were doing, the plant life was definitely winning.

Foxy turned on her heel, getting the feeling that that was not a battle she wanted to join. Instead, she headed toward the horse barn. Inside, she could hear her soon-to-be brother-in-law barking orders as was the Matthews boys' way.

Even before the lot joined the Armed Forces, they all spoke in commands that they expected others to immediately obey. Peeking inside the barn, Foxy saw the recipient of those commands was the most ornery foster kid of the bunch. True to form, Denny was as combative as ever.

"They're not listening to me," said Denny.

"You have to show them who's boss," said Charlie.

"I thought you were the boss."

Foxy failed to hide a giggle as she watched the two face off. Denny was as lanky as Joe had been when they were kids. But unlike Joe, who always had a thoughtful expression, like he was doing math in his head, Denny wore a perpetual scowl.

As always, Charlie Matthews was calm and in command. Foxy doubted it even occurred to him that someone would disobey a direct order from him. "You need to make sure the horse is aware of you."

"He can see me," said Denny. "He still won't lift his foot."

"Run your hand down his leg. Then squeeze the tendon."

"The what?"

"The place above his ankle—yes, that's it. Now he'll lift his own foot."

There was a spark of triumph in Denny's eyes as the horse did as he commanded. When the kid looked up, he was met with the same spark in Charlie's eyes. So of course, being ornery, Denny wiped the triumphant look from his face and replaced it with a scowl.

And of course, Charlie being certain that his orders would always be followed, the former pilot gave a self-satisfied nod at the kid and the horse. "Now, you can remove the shoe with the tools. Hey, Foxy. How'd it go with your old boss?"

"He said no."

Charlie wrinkled his nose, giving Foxy a clenched half-smile.

"But someone else said yes," Foxy said, stepping up to one of the stalls and petting the head of the horse that poked its nose over the gate.

"Oh?" Charlie's eyes went wide, and the half-smile rounded into an O of surprise.

"What? You didn't think I would get them?"

Charlie shrugged, his good-natured smile slipping back in place. "Well, you do leave an impression wherever you go."

Foxy decided to ignore the quip. She and Charlie poked at each other like brother and sister since they were foster care kids. In fact, all the Matthews boys treated her that way, except one. Joe never poked or prodded. He'd always stood by, making sure she didn't get into too big of a scrape or dusting her off if he hadn't gotten to her in time.

"You'll never guess who I ran into while I was getting the recommendation?"

"Just tell me," said Charlie, as he turned his attention back to Denny and the horse. "You know I hate guessing. I'm not psychic."

Foxy gritted her teeth at the P-word, knowing Charlie only said it to get a rise out of her. "I saw Joe."

"Joe came to find you?"

"No. Why would he come to find me? He was on a date."

"Joe was on a date? With another woman?"

"Another woman? Is he dating more than one? He just got back into town."

Charlie stared at her dumbly.

Foxy got the sense that she was missing something. Whatever it was that went over her head, the gut feeling she'd gotten when Joe had come into Charlotte's offices was much better gossip. "The woman Joe's out with now, I think she might be the one."

"You do? Your psychic powers tell you that?" Charlie's tone was doubtful, but all Foxy heard was the P-word. She wouldn't ignore it this time.

"I'm not psychic," she hissed through clenched teeth.

"Yeah, I'll say."

"I'm clairsentient. It means I get feelings that—"

"Mr. Charlie, I'm done. Can I go now?"

"Denny, you know better than to interrupt adults when they're talking," said Charlie.

Denny rubbed at his temple. The kid looked a little green behind the gills. Foxy reached for Denny's hand to tug him out of the stall. The moment her fingers touched his, she got a sharp pain in her gut.

"Denny? What's wrong? Are you not feeling well?"

Denny pursed his lips. He looked from Foxy to Charlie and then down at the ground. "It's nothing."

"It's not nothing," said Foxy, gripping his hand tighter. She knew that much in her gut. If it was nothing, her gut would be quiet. If it was something good, there'd be a tingling warmth. Instead, her stomach growled and grumbled like she was going to be sick.

"I'm not sick," Denny said finally." But I… you'll think I'm crazy."

"Everybody thinks I'm crazy because I get these feelings I can't always explain."

"I have a feeling, a bad feeling."

Foxy waited patiently for Denny to finish. The more seconds that ticked by, she grew certain that she knew what he was about to say.

"It's Daria. I have a bad feeling she's in trouble."

"You got your law degree at the University of Montana Western? I went to Montana State Northern. What a coincidence."

Joe blinked, but the motion didn't bring the woman sitting across from him into focus. In his mind's eye, he'd been replaying the reunion with Foxy over and over again. His arms tingling as they'd tightened around her. His fingers aching where they'd come in contact with her soft, warm flesh. He wanted to shove away the chicken dish, whose herbaceous aroma was muddling his memory of Foxy's sweet and fruity smell.

"My goal has always been to earn partner by the time I'm thirty. At my old firm, I got there just a couple of years early. Then I left and opened my own firm."

Joe blinked again, bringing Charlotte O'Dell into focus. It was the woman's ambition that finally wrangled some of his attention away from Foxy and to his lunch date. Joe had had a similar ambition to Charlotte when he'd first started law school. Though instead of making partner in a law firm, he'd risen to the highest rank a lawyer could in the military as a JAG. Now his sights were set on becoming a District Attorney. Maybe one day Attorney General.

"I had thought I wanted to become an A.G. one day," Charlotte was saying. "But I like my work too much."

"You practice family law?" asked Joe, at last pulling his own weight in the conversation. If Charlotte noticed the inequity, she didn't say.

"I do," Charlotte said after taking a sip of her sparkling water. "My family is amazing. My mom stayed home and did the traditional wife thing. Dad was the breadwinner, but he was home every night for dinner, at every after-school game or function. I remember looking up around the lunchroom at school one day and realizing not every kid had what I had, and wasn't that a shame."

If there was one thing that Joe could not abide, it was do-gooders offering pity or handouts. That wasn't Charlotte. He could see it in her crystal clear blue eyes. Charlotte's palm wasn't open. It was balled into a fist. Like she wanted to knock out the injustice she witnessed in the family courts.

"It never occurred to me that anyone would take advantage of a child," Charlotte said. "Not their parents. Or worse, their own government. Someone needs to be their champion."

A tendril of sunlight snuck into the window from behind the curtains. It made its way across the floor and up the table. That single ray landed on the side of Charlotte's wrist. When she moved her hand to lift a slice of strawberry from her fruit salad, the clouds shifted, and the light was gone.

"I'm a practical woman, Captain Matthews."

"Joe. I told you to call me Joe." Joe looked up into the sky. The sun was still there in muted yellow. If he waited a while longer, it would surely shift back and shine its light inside the restaurant again.

"Because I'm a friend of Foxy James?"

Joe shifted his gaze from the window to the woman. Charlotte's blue eyes pierced him like a prosecutor who sniffed a confession that was forthcoming.

"She's a character, that one," Charlotte continued in Joe's silence.

"That she is," Joe agreed, cutting into a slice of his chicken dish.

"So, the two of you…"

"The two of us?" Joe speared the slice of meat onto his fork. "No. We're… not."

"When she ran into your arms back in my office, and you held on so tightly for so long, I thought…"

Joe waited a beat before he spoke. When Charlotte held back what she thought of him and Foxy, he filled in the blank.

"We're childhood friends. I haven't seen her in years."

"About nine years? Three thousand, five hundred and sixty-seven days to be exact."

"I have a thing for numbers."

Charlotte grinned, but there was censure behind that smile. Her walls were up. Joe knew that with the right words, he could knock them down.

"There's nothing between me and Foxy."

It hurt his tongue to say it. But it was the truth. It was just an old childhood crush. Foxy didn't even think of him that way. Not then. Not now. He had to get over this.

Before him sat a woman who was perfect for

him. And despite his poor behavior on this date, she still showed interest in him.

"I'm glad to hear that there's nothing between you and her." Charlotte moved another strawberry from her salad and speared a mandarin orange instead. "She doesn't seem your type."

"My type?"

"You seem like the kind of man that needs a serious woman on your arm."

"A serious woman like you?"

"Why not? Foxy seemed to think so. I think she was going to try to match us together before you walked in the door."

It should not hurt. But it did.

"She fancies herself a psychic."

"She's not psychic. She's clairsentient." Joe sat his knife and fork down. The sliced and diced piece of chicken untouched. "She gets feelings. But they're not always clear, and they're not always right. Sometimes she gets things wrong."

"Do you think she could be right about us?"

Charlotte sat her fork and knife down. All the fruit in the bowl gone except the strawberries. She fit the bill for the perfect political wife.

"I think the two of us could make a great partnership, Joe. We would be assets to each other's careers."

There it was. A clear, logical plan. Something quantitative that he could measure. It did not matter that she didn't make his heart skip beats when he looked at her. Not only would the woman be good for his career, she would be good for his health, too.

Joe paid for the meal after a cursory tug of war with Charlotte over the check. She might be a successful career woman, which Joe definitely found attractive, but she was also from a traditional household, which Joe craved in a woman. Then they were outside the restaurant, gazing awkwardly at each other.

Joe leaned in. However, it was just as Charlotte reached out her hand, palm up, for a shake. Quickly, she withdrew her hand and tilted her head up. Unfortunately, it was as Joe thrust his hand out and just barely missed groping her chest.

They laughed. The sound burst from them in awkward gasps. Then there was silence. Finally, Joe leaned down and pressed a peck on Charlotte's cheek.

"You'll call me?" she said.

"I'll call you," he agreed.

Hopping in his car, Joe took off toward home. That kiss had sealed the deal for him. He'd closed off his past and decided he was taking his future in both of his hands.

Charlotte was the right choice. The logical choice. That was the only choice since Foxy didn't feel about him the way he felt about her.

With his future decided, Joe took a left turn to head toward Rich's place in town. It would be better if he stayed there the night instead of on the ranch where he'd be too near temptation. And so Joe cut a U-turn and drove toward the sun, which would lead him away from his homestead.

He had to blink a couple of times when he saw the rainbow-colored van on the side of the road. By the third blink, recognition dawned. It was the Bright Horizons Foster Care van. When he had ridden in that van as a child, it had been a dull yellow. The James sisters had since painted the old jalopy in bright shades to befit the home's name.

Beneath the hood of the van, he saw a shapely figure. Joe didn't remember telling his foot to press the brake. He didn't remember hopping out of the car and coming to her side.

"Thank the saints you saw me," said Foxy when he came up to her. "It just stopped working."

"Have you taken it in for regular maintenance?"

"I was going to, but my gut told me I'd be okay. And I am because here you are."

Joe opened his mouth to protest the warnings of a check engine light—which was on—and the grumblings of an upset stomach. He knew that with this woman, it would be a moot point. The words came up regardless.

"You have to keep a regular repair schedule if you want your car to remain dependable."

"Something important came up," Foxy said.

"More important than your safety? Or one of the kids' safety? What if one of the foster kids had been in the van with you?"

"That's what this is about. It's about one of the foster kids. My gut tells me that one of them is in trouble."

Joe pursed his lips. So much of his past mishaps started with this woman saying those words; *my gut told me.*

"I just want to check on her," she said. "She's at the state home."

"That's an hour's drive."

"Will you give me a ride?"

"You should call your sister and have her pick you up."

"There's no time. Visiting hours will be over soon and... Joe, I've got a bad feeling."

He should say no. He should call Savy, or his brother, to come and deal with this. He should take Foxy home himself. This situation could easily be handled with a phone call or on the next day.

Instead of doing any of that, Joe said, "Okay, hop in."

CHAPTER EIGHT

Foxy gazed out the passenger side window as the sun slipped lower in the sky. The city skyline gave way to open fields as the miles clicked away. There was a warm glow outside of the car in the sinking sunlight. Inside the car, it felt as though storm clouds were moving in.

Joe sat in the driver's seat, silent and tense. It would have alarmed her if it was anyone else. But it was Joe. And this was his normal stasis.

He'd always been a quiet kid. Thoughtful. Only speaking when he was asked to provide an answer. Or speaking up when he saw an injustice taking place. Joe was not one to stand silent when someone was doing something wrong. Be it his brothers or the James sisters. He was the group's conscience.

Even when he stood silently by them, everyone would always think twice about their actions under Joe's watchful gaze.

His gaze was on the road now. That strong jaw of his ticked, as though he wanted to say something but wouldn't. Why wouldn't he speak his peace to her? They were still friends, even after all these years.

"Bad date?" Foxy asked when she could take the silence no more.

"I'm sorry, what?" Joe squinted, but he didn't take his eyes off the road.

"With Charlotte? Did you have a bad date?"

He opened his mouth, then closed it. Foxy couldn't get a feel for what he had been about to say. She didn't need her gut to tell her what had happened earlier. Her feminine sensibilities told her that the date had not gone so well.

"Don't worry about it," Foxy soothed. "It doesn't always take the first time."

"What doesn't always take the first time?"

"True love," she said. "It doesn't always happen at first sight."

Joe's gaze left the empty road and turned to her. His lips parted. His eyes wide as he took her in.

There was surprise on his handsome face. Just as

soon as Foxy named the emotion, his expression changed. Joe's lips pinched together. His fingers gripped the steering wheel. With the way he looked at her now, Foxy felt like she had just committed a grave injustice. But against whom?

"Love takes its own time to grow," she assured him. "Trust me. I've been waiting for my true love to show up for years. He's super late. But I'm trying to be patient."

"Right," Joe scoffed. "Your true love. Your mystery hero."

Foxy nodded, pleased that he remembered the vision she'd told him she'd had when she was young. "He's going to show up in my greatest time of need."

Joe rolled his eyes and turned back to face the road. The pinched expression remained in his eyes and his lips. He shook his head and muttered something under his breath. It sounded like he might've said *unbelievable.*

"What?" Foxy cocked her head, swiveling in her seat to face him. "I thought you believed in my gift."

"I've never believed in extrasensory perception," he said. At least he didn't insult her by calling her a psychic. "We have five senses that make up reality. The most prevalent one being sight and seeing what's right in front of your face."

"Light is energy. Energy that your eyes interpret as colors and depth to form an image. Feelings are also energy; electrochemical energy, which the mind makes interpretations of."

How did Foxy know that technical, scientific definition of her abilities? Because Joe had looked it up in a textbook at the library and explained it to her after some kids made fun of her. Of course, back then, when she'd tried to explain that to the juvenile delinquents in the face of their taunts, they'd only jeered at her even more.

"I seem to remember," Joe was saying, "that every time you got one of your feelings, I was the one that wound up coming face to face with reality."

"What are you talking about?" said Foxy.

"Like that time in elementary school, when you got the feeling that if you climbed to the top of the monkey bars and sang, it would push the gray clouds away."

"It did. Though just not exactly how I imagined it. Mrs. Reed had been sad, and when I sang, she was happy."

"Before you finished the song, you lost your balance and fell."

"And you caught me."

"That's my point. You got a feeling, and I faced

the reality. Like that time you got a feeling that a spirit was in the closet at the foster home."

Foxy winced at that memory. There hadn't been a spirit there. Will Matthews had put a Chucky doll in there after they'd snuck into the theater one Halloween to watch the horror film.

"When I opened the door for you, and Chucky fell down from the heap, you knocked me down in your effort to get away, and I wound up with stitches."

"Yeah, but it was a really good scar. Will and Charlie were envious of you."

Foxy could see remnants of the outline just above Joe's temple. She reached her hand up to touch it. As her fingers brushed Joe's temple, his body tensed. Sensation flooded her finger when she connected with his warm skin. More memories of their time as children came tumbling back into her mind.

"You were always there for me. No matter how out there my visions were."

Joe didn't answer. He held his breath. He kept his eyes on the road.

Foxy remembered Joe hadn't liked being touched as a kid. It was a common occurrence with kids who had been abandoned by their birth parents. As far as she knew, she was the only person Joe had allowed this kind of contact. So, she took liberties.

Foxy brushed her thumb over the scar. Her palm tingled where it met the sharp angle of Joe's cheekbone. His jaw tightened and then relaxed in her hold. Just as she had when she was a child, Foxy felt a profound sense of gratitude that she could bring him comfort.

"I'm glad you're home. You're going to make a great District Attorney."

He shut his eyes. Only briefly. In that brief moment, Foxy felt the weight of the world lift from his shoulders.

Joe was a crusader for justice. It was one of the things she loved about her friend. He would need someone there to shoulder that weight.

"Charlotte is the perfect political girlfriend," said Foxy.

She supposed that someone would be Charlotte O'Dell. The lawyer would understand Joe's trials and tribulations far better than Foxy ever would. But Foxy would still be there for her friend to help him, not take everything so seriously.

Joe pulled away from her touch then. "What makes you say that about Charlotte?"

"You're both lawyers. Both crusaders for justice.

You both will take on a case for the underdog. You two will probably change the world together."

Foxy folded her hand down into her lap. It still tingled with the reminder of Joe's warmth. She balled her fingers into a fist, trying to hold on to some of that warmth.

"Don't worry," she said. "I'll stay in the shadows, so no one sees your woo-woo psychic friend."

"You weren't meant for the shadows, Fox. You're too bright."

There was a spark in Joe's eyes as he turned back to her. His gazed roamed over her features. The embers in his hazel eyes were so bright they reminded Foxy of sparklers.

A match struck in her gut. So loud she swore she heard it in her ears. The flame inside her caught quick, so hot it burned its way up her chest and scorched the recesses of her heart. "You shouldn't be looking at me like that, dear."

"Why not?"

Had Joe's voice always been that deep? Like a sleeping bear roused in the dead of winter looking for his next meal?

"Why not?" he repeated, his hot gaze still on her.

It took Foxy's muddled brain another second to figure out the answer to Joe's question. From the corner of her eye, she saw the meaning of the gut-check.

"Joe, there's a deer."

Everything happened in a split second, but time appeared to slow to Foxy. She saw as the fire in Joe's eyes was snuffed out and replaced with fear. She saw the tips of his fingers turn first red with blood, then white when the blood drained as he put a death grip on the steering wheel. Joe's right forearm reached out and slammed into Foxy's chest, holding her back as he floored the brakes, and they both crashed forward into the dashboard of the car.

CHAPTER NINE

A light flashed before Joe's eyes. The light was bright, but it did not blind him. He saw everything clearly. In the moment before Joe Matthews thought he would die, all he saw was Foxy James.

Foxy singing at the top of her lungs from the playground monkey bars.

Foxy grabbing his hand and telling him to come with her on an adventure.

Foxy smiling up at him as she taught him how to dance the two-step before the middle school dance.

Foxy in tears when she'd learned that her mother had returned to take her and her sisters away. Foxy, the most spirited person he had ever met, looking up at him with an expression of helplessness. Foxy sighing softly as he pressed his lips so carefully, so gently to hers. Foxy closing her eyes and resting her head against his shoulder after sharing their first kiss.

She'd fallen asleep in his arms that night. In the morning, she was gone. Her mother had come to get her to take her and her sisters out on the road as her backup singers. He hadn't seen her again after that moment.

Foxy's eyes were closed right now. Her hand pressed to her forehead. Her beautiful features contorted into a grimace of pain.

Joe threw off his seatbelt to reach for her. He ignored the protest of the bruises forming on his arm as he did so. Somehow, Joe had survived not being near her for the last few years. What he could not bear was to be in a world where she didn't exist.

"Don't move," he insisted. "There could be internal damage."

"I'm fine," Foxy insisted. But the words were said through clenched teeth. "It's just a bump on the head."

"It could be a concussion." Joe took her head in his hands. Then he commanded, "Open your eyes for me."

Foxy did as he asked. For a moment, Joe could

only stare dumbfounded. Firstly, because no James sister did what she was commanded to do. Secondly, because she looked up at him with tears in her eyes. Her expression was helpless, just as it had been all those years ago when he'd had his first taste of heaven.

Joe stared into Foxy's eyes. Foxy stared back at him. They were close enough to repeat that kiss. Joe could even taste the berry sweetness of her breath.

Foxy reached for him. Her fingers brushing his temple for the second time today. Just like he'd done earlier, Joe closed his eyes at her touch and let himself get lost in the dream. When her fingertips met his forehead, he felt something warm, wet, and sticky.

Joe opened his eyes to find that Foxy wasn't lost in a dream like he was. She was staring in horror at the blood on her hands. His blood.

"You're hurt," she said.

He was hurt. Hurt that she didn't remember what had happened between them. Hurt that she wouldn't even acknowledge the kiss that they'd shared. Hurt that she still searched for her true love, the man who was supposed to be there at the most difficult moment in her life when he had been the one there for her when her life had been turned upside down. Angry with himself that even after all of that, he could not walk away from her.

"Joe, you're bleeding."

"I'm fine."

"You threw your arm out to protect me."

"Of course, I did."

She reached for him again. Joe dodged her touch. He couldn't bear another friendly touch from the woman he craved. Not when she showed no signs of hunger for him.

Instead, he turned away from Foxy and climbed out of the car to inspect the damage. She'd called him dear. But that had been a misinterpretation.

A deer had run into the road a second before Foxy had warned him. Joe had swerved, but the motion drove them off the road and landed them in a ditch. The back wheels of the car were not touching pavement. Joe was able to get out, but the car was well and truly stuck.

"Stay here," Joe told Foxy as he pulled out his cell phone.

He held the device up to the darkening sky. Not a single bar of service joined him under the setting sun. There was no reception out here in the middle of nowhere.

The bars left him stranded, but Foxy was

preparing to join him. The passenger side door creaked open as she tried to emerge. Joe was around the car before Foxy was all the way out.

"I told you to stay put," he admonished. "You might be injured."

"I'm fine. You're the one who's hurt."

Foxy wobbled as she stood. Joe pulled her to him. They stood there for a moment, chest to chest, gazes locked. Heat coerced up and down his forearms where he caged her in. Foxy's lips parted, and a gasp escaped. Her nostrils flared, but her gaze narrowed in clear confusion. She still didn't get it. Instead of pushing her away, Joe pulled her closer.

"If anything would've happened to you..." He couldn't finish the sentence. He couldn't voice the thought. Luckily, she did it for him.

"If anything would've happened to me, my sister would've killed you."

Joe grinned at that. Foxy mirrored his smile. Her hands rested on his chest, right where his heart beat out an erratic rhythm for her.

They were still standing so close. Almost like an embrace. Exactly like when she'd taught him to dance in preparation for the school function. His hands were at her hips. Her hands were pressed against his chest. They weren't swaying, but the world around them seemed to be.

"Déjà vu," she said.

"Are you remembering teaching me how to dance?"

Foxy nodded. "You were pitiful."

"Blame it on my teacher," he said.

There was a slight wind drifting past them as dusk began to settle. Slowly, they began to sway in time to the breeze.

"I've gotten better since then," Joe said as they swayed to the right.

"I'm sure you have," Foxy said as they swayed to the left.

"Fox..."

Foxy dipped her forehead and rested it against his chest. Joe's arms instantly closed around her.

"My head is so foggy," she said. "My emotions and feelings are all over the place. I can't think straight."

That's exactly how Joe felt every time he thought of her. Foxy was always telling others about her feelings. For once in his life, he needed to tell her how he felt.

They'd stopped swaying and were still now. The wind continued to whisper between them. The words Joe wanted to say were on the tip of his tongue. They were nearly out of his mouth when the sound of a loud motor and a honking horse broke the silence he'd been about to fill.

"You two okay?" called a gruff voice from the driver's side window.

Joe turned to see an old couple in a beat-up pickup truck pull to a stop beside them.

"You're not going to get a tow truck out here until morning," said the old man in the driver's seat. "You can come stay with us until then."

CHAPTER TEN

There were streamers in her memory. The theme of the dance all those years ago had been Enchanted Forest. Foxy knew she had danced all night long with each boy in her class. The funny thing was the only face she could remember swaying in time to the slow beat with her was Joe's.

The dance lessons had been awful. Joe had stepped on her foot with his left foot, then again with his right foot. She didn't remember a single second of the pain from her toes.

All Foxy could remember was how the two of them had laughed. How big Joe had smiled. How safe and secure she'd felt in his arms, even as her toes had been at the height of danger.

At the dance, there hadn't been any laughing or

joking. He hadn't stepped on her toes a single time. Even while she'd made the rounds with other boys in the class, Joe hadn't danced with any other girl.

Again and again, Foxy had gravitated back to him with every slow song. Though she'd been abandoned as a child like Joe, she had never had any hang-ups about being touched. Still, no one had ever made her feel as grounded and steady as Joe Matthews.

Even in the midst of the car crash, Foxy had known that Joe would take care of her. As evidenced by the forearm he'd flung out to protect her. She knew he had to be bruised as well as bloodied. It wouldn't be the first time he'd put himself in harm's way for her.

Joe would never let anything bad happen to her. Even the times when he hadn't been able to protect her, thoughts of him and his steady smile had always reminded Foxy of the good in this world.

Joe wasn't smiling now. He wasn't even looking at her as they sat in the back of the pickup truck. As the older couple ambled down the long, deserted road, Foxy let Joe speak for them all the way until they reached their farmhouse. She let Joe take care of scheduling a tow truck in the morning. She let Joe call their family and tell them where they were and that they were fine.

"We only have the one room," said Mr. Drummond, the old farmer who had happened upon them on the side of the road.

Joe stopped walking. That would've been fine if they weren't on the stairs and Foxy wasn't walking behind him. She bumped right into his broad back, his broad back that was ripe with muscles. With all those muscles, Foxy would've expected him to be hard planes. Instead, she walked into the center of his back and fell into the same cushion that was at the front of his chest. Instead of instantly stepping back, Foxy reached her hand around to the front of Joe's waist. She told herself it was to steady herself, but when she met with even more muscles at his abs, her brain momentarily fried. Instead of letting go, she got it in her mind to count the number of abs she found.

Yep, it was a six-pack.

"One room is fine," Joe said as he unfurled her fingers and removed her hands from his waist. "We were raised together. Like brother and sister."

The words tasted like sandpaper as Foxy said them silently to herself. Joe continued up the stairs, leaving her standing there. She felt cold in her belly, the premonition that something was off. But she couldn't tell what.

Joe only had a bruise after he'd let Mrs. Drummond clean up the cut on his forehead. Neither of them were exhibiting any of the signs of a concussion. So what was wrong?

"You take the bed," said Joe once the door was closed behind them.

Those words felt wrong as well. The cold sensation in the pit of her belly increased. Foxy realized the last thing she wanted was to have any distance between herself and Joe. She wanted him to hold her close like when they were kids.

"Joe, we can share the bed. It wouldn't be the first time."

"We were kids back then. We're not kids anymore."

"What?" Foxy scoffed. "It's not like you're going to ravish me?"

Joe didn't laugh at the joke. Foxy wasn't laughing, either. That coldness in her belly was starting to spread. She knew what would make it go away, another one of Joe's warm, secure hugs.

"Tell me something…"

Foxy waited for Joe's question. It took him a moment to formulate it. His jaw working as though he wasn't sure if he wanted the words to get out. Which was odd. Didn't he know he could tell her anything?

"Why are you so sure about me and Charlotte?" was what he finally asked.

"Because of the feeling."

"What did you feel?"

Foxy searched for the words. It was always hard to convey the sensations she felt in her gut. "A rightness. An inevitability. It's the same thing I feel when I think about my true love. I felt that feeling when you and Charlotte were in the room together earlier."

"Maybe it was Charlotte and Richard?"

"No." Foxy shook her head, the warmth of certainty returning to her belly. "It was for you."

Joe was quiet for a long time. Then he sat down on the edge of the bed. Foxy came over and sat next to him.

"Did you ever think…" He stopped and cleared his throat. "Maybe it was for the two of us?"

Foxy smiled at that. "I've always felt a rightness with you. Whenever you would give me a hug, even as a kid, I've never felt more safe and secure."

"But not romantic?"

"Joe, you know I'm saving myself for my true

love. There's never been anything romantic between me and any other guy."

"What about when we kissed?"

Foxy's mouth fell open. She was so surprised that she had to try a couple of times before she could get any words out. "We never kissed."

Now it was Joe's mouth that fell open. "You really don't remember, do you?"

"Remember what?"

"It doesn't matter." Joe huffed through his nose and rose from the bed.

"Where are you going?"

"You're psychic, can't you guess? Can't you feel it?" He turned and glared at her before going out the door. "I'm going to sleep on the couch downstairs."

Foxy wanted to reach out to him, to call him back. But she lost her voice. The coldness in her stomach came back and snatched all the warmth Joe's nearness had brought.

What had that been all about? What kiss? She'd never kissed anyone before, let alone her closest friend?

So why did the denial of that increase the chill in her gut?

CHAPTER ELEVEN

"An accident? Wait, where are you?"

Joe held the phone away from his ear. How was it that the rotary landline phone was loud and crisp and made Rich sound like he was shouting right beside him? It had taken three tries as the old dial up rang and rang before Rich even picked up his cell phone to answer the unknown and unlisted number.

"I'm on Route 29."

"What are you doing out there in the middle of nowhere?" asked Rich. He wasn't shouting this time, just speaking at his normal volume, but his voice still boomed in Joe's ear. Likely a side effect from bumping his head on the dash.

"I had some business to attend to." Joe looked up

at the stairs where Foxy was resting her pretty head behind a closed door while he cleaned up the mess.

Here he was again. She got one of her visions or feelings, and he got the short end of the stick. Joe rubbed at his head. His fingertip bumped the band aid Mrs. Drummond had placed there. The blood flow had long stopped, but a bruise had formed under the bandage. Rich would have a literal cow when he saw it. It would certainly mess up the publicity photos he had planned for this weekend.

"What kind of business?" asked Rich.

"Family business," said Joe.

Because that was all he was to Foxy. Just a surrogate brother who was always there to catch her when she wasn't looking where she was going. Which was every single day. How had the woman survived without him all these years?

There hadn't been another man in her life. He knew that now, after she confessed that she was still waiting on her soul mate's arrival. And since Joe was not him, Foxy didn't even remember the kiss they'd shared all those years ago.

Whereas Joe had thought of Foxy every day. Nearly every second of every day. To the point where her name had been doodled on court dockets a time or two.

The imaginary Foxy had been his happy place. It was the live one who caused him pain. Especially now that he knew that she wasn't pretending the kiss never happened. She truly didn't remember it.

Joe remembered every second of it. Every scent. Every sigh. Every single one of her eyelashes as they'd brushed against his cheek.

There had been tears at the corners of her eyes as she'd hid from the adults when her mother arrived. Foxy had had a bad feeling for days, but she couldn't pinpoint where it came from. She wouldn't leave her room, fearing the monster was coming to the door and not hiding under the bed or in the closet. When she learned who the monster was, she'd called out for Joe. She'd sat huddled in his arms as the moments to her departure ticked down.

The sun rose and set, and he held her.

The moments ticked by, becoming hours, and he held her.

At one point, Foxy had looked up at Joe with those long lashes, the scent of strawberries on her breath, and her lips had brushed his.

So softly. Just for a heartbeat. Joe's entire world had changed in the space of that heartbeat.

When he opened his eyes, hers were closed. She tucked her head into the crook of his neck and went to sleep. Soon after, he followed her into dreamland. When he woke, she was gone.

"I'd hoped you were spending more time with Charlotte," Rich's voice boomed from the phone. "She said the date went well, and she thinks it can be a great partnership."

"Yeah, about Charlotte."

"She's great, isn't she? I told you she's perfect."

"She is. Perfect for me."

"I'll check with her people to see if she can make the photoshoot this weekend."

"No, don't do that."

"Why not?"

"Charlotte's not the one."

"You just said yourself, she's perfect."

"She is."

"Man, you're not making any sense."

"Matters of the heart rarely do." Joe rubbed at the bruise on his forehead. "Charlotte's a good woman. She deserves a good man."

"You're a good man. You're the best man I know."

"I can't love her. It would be wrong to pretend."

Rich let out a long sigh over the phone. He knew better than to argue with Joe when the decorated soldier and lawyer brought up right and wrong.

"I'm just going to be a bachelor candidate," said

Joe. "On the bright side, the society pages will splash my eligibility all over the gossip pages. That'll keep me in the press."

"That could work." Joe couldn't see his friend, but he could all but hear Rich stroking his chin like a dastardly villain formulating his master plan. "You just need to stay out of the tabloids. Wait, look who I'm talking to. You are a veritable Boy Scout."

"Eagle Scout," Joe corrected. He was the only one of his brothers that had stuck through the Scouting program to earn his wings.

"All right, Eagle Man. We'll move the announcement of your candidacy to tomorrow night. Do you need me to send you a car to get you home?"

"No, it's fine. Don't go out of your way. I'm in a safe place, and they'll have my car ready in the morning."

After a few more instructions and a couple more tries to get Joe to reconsider a relationship with Charlotte, Rich let him go. Joe slipped the phone back onto its holder base. He looked up at the darkened staircase.

There hadn't been a peep from Foxy, which was not usual. If Joe was a veritable Eagle Scout, Foxy was a twittering parrot. Quiet was not her modus operandi.

He supposed she was sleeping.

But she did get bumped on the head.

She might have a concussion.

From his time in sports and his military training, Joe knew that protocol was to wake a concussed person every three to four hours.

Joe looked at his watch. It hadn't been an hour yet. She also might not be asleep just yet. He should make sure he would be starting the countdown from the right hour, lest he wake her just as she went to sleep in three hours.

Joe placed his foot on the first rung of the stair. It held his weight silently. It was the third step that creaked and announced his intentions.

Mrs. Drummond poked her head out of the kitchen, a washrag in her hand, a curious expression on her face.

"I'm just going to check on her," said Joe. "She might have a concussion. You're supposed to wake a concussed person every few hours."

Mrs. Drummond nodded. "You're a good brother."

Joe sighed at the characterization. He was tired of being cast as Foxy James's friend or surrogate brother. But if that's how he was going to stay in her life, then he'd swallow the bitter pill. Because his heart simply wasn't interested in trying to find sweetness in another woman.

He knocked quietly on the door. When there was no response, he pushed it open. Foxy lay on the bed. Joe came to the side of the bed and stared for a moment. One arm was flung over her head, the other lay off to the side. The white sheets bunched up around her, making her look like a fallen angel.

"Joe?" Foxy spoke without opening her eyes.

"I thought you were sleeping."

"I was, but I felt your energy." She opened her eyes and stared up at him. There were unshed tears in those beautiful eyes. "I don't understand why you're angry at me."

"I lost you back there."

It was an understatement. He'd almost lost her in that car accident. He had truly lost her when he realized she did not, and likely would never, feel the way about him that he felt about her.

"You would never lose me," Foxy said. "You're my safe place."

She reached out her hand to him. Joe took it. He took her hand, and he took those words, unable to keep himself from grasping at any straw she gave to him.

Joe climbed atop the mattress. He stretched out

his body, laying on top of the sheets that the woman for whom his heartbeat lay under. Foxy curled his arm around her. She lay her head down in the crook of his elbow and went back to sleep.

It took only a few moments, but with the steady pace of her heartbeats and the even sighs of her breath, Joe allowed himself to be lulled to sleep. He did not wake himself or her in three hours. If they were both concussed, he'd rather stay wrapped up in this dreamworld than wake.

CHAPTER TWELVE

It was the best sleep Foxy had had in days, weeks, years. It was so soul reviving. It was spirit-lifting. It was so safe, secure, filling her with so much love and warmth that she didn't want to leave it.

It was also not like any other dream she'd ever had. She didn't see anything in the dream. Just a peaceful darkness. It was the feel of the dream that Foxy didn't want to part with.

It felt like a homecoming. It felt right. It felt inevitable.

It was like the times she dreamed about her true love. She hadn't had that dream in a long time. Having it now must mean he was near. It must mean that she was going to meet him soon. Maybe even today.

In her mind, Foxy's eyes flew open, eager to greet this momentous day. In reality, her eyelids lifted slowly, shirking away from the soft sunlight that peeked behind the curtains. With only one eye open, a toasty brown chest was revealed to her.

Foxy was lying in someone's arms.

As she moved from dream world to real life, the feelings didn't leave. Inside these arms, Foxy felt the same safety. She felt completely secure, as though these arms would never let her fall. It felt right having her body alongside this stranger's.

When she lifted her head, she wasn't surprised to see Joe gazing down at her. As one of her oldest and closest friends, Joe had always been a safe space for her. But he wasn't her dream man. He wasn't her soul mate. She would've known that years ago.

Foxy blinked the crust out of her eyes. There was no sleep crud in her eyes. She squinted, but there was no need. She saw things clearly.

Joe's handsome face stayed in focus. The feelings of security, safety, and warmth remained. Her heart insisted this was where it wanted to be. Her gut was a calm sea of tranquility.

What was going on with her?

It was then that Foxy glanced at Joe's mouth. Those lips were a soft pink pillow she wanted to rest her own lips against. The urge was so sudden, so palpable, that it took her by surprise. The surprise took her back years ago to a dream she once had. A dream where she kissed her true love good night and fell asleep in his arms.

Only that wasn't a dream. That had happened.

The last night she'd spent as a ward of the state at the Bright Horizon's foster home, Joe had slept in her bed. She'd been terrified at what life would bring her when her mother came to collect her and her sisters in the morning. As always, Joe was there.

He'd been there with her all day, as she'd stayed cooped up in her room. He'd been there with her all night, as she'd refused to leave her bed. Joe had simply sat beside her as silent tears fell. Then he'd held her as she fell asleep. But not before Foxy had tilted up her head and brushed her lips against his.

Holy stars, she had kissed Joe Matthews.

She hadn't meant to kiss him. She'd only meant to say thank you. Only her lips hadn't formed the words. The brush of his lips against hers had said all she'd needed to say, and then she'd fallen asleep. The same contented sleep she'd just experienced now. And when she woke from a night surrounded by his strength, she'd felt strong enough to face the new reality of her life.

How had she forgotten that? How had she forgotten him? How had she not remembered that the silent strength she'd carried around from that day had been from Joe?

"It's you?" she said.

Joe's eyes were open, wide open. His nostrils flared at her words. His heart skipped a beat. Foxy knew because her hand rested on his strong chest.

Foxy shifted in Joe's arms so that she could take all of him in. There was the strong chin that could argue a case if it would lead to justice being done. There were the bright hazel eyes that had watched over her, looking out for any sign of danger as she blindly dashed into the fray to deliver her own brand of justice that came from her gut. There were those two soft lips that always spoke up for her, even when he didn't agree with, or even understand, what she went on about.

"You're my true love?" Foxy couldn't stop the question mark from tagging along at the end of that sentence. Her gut was sure. Her heart was onboard. It was her head that was foggy. How had she not seen this so clearly?

For his part, Joe's features were screwed as he

looked down at her. "Are you asking me or telling me?"

"How could I have not seen this?" Foxy sat up in the bed, the sheets falling away from her body to reveal that she'd fallen asleep in yesterday's clothing.

Joe sat up as well, resting his back against the headboard of the bed. "I've been asking myself the same thing for years."

"Years?" Foxy reared back and gaped at him. "You've known this for years, and you didn't tell me. How could you keep this from me?"

"Me? How could I…? Me?"

"Yes, you." She jabbed a finger in his chest. "We're supposed to be friends, and you didn't tell me you were my one true love."

"This is my fault?" Joe jabbed his own finger at his chest. "How is this my fault? Aren't you the one who's supposed to be psychic?"

Foxy threw her hands up in the air in exasperation. "I'm not psychic."

"I know, I know. You're clairsentient. You feel things." Joe motioned his hand over his heart."

"It's in the gut," Foxy corrected, but he wasn't paying attention.

"Except when someone has feelings for you.

Then you block it out and forget that it ever happened."

"But you felt it." Foxy rose to her knees on the mattress so that she could tower over him. She only came up to his chin. "I can't believe you, Joe Matthews. We wasted all this time when we could've been..."

"When we could've been what?"

Joe came to his knees as well. Foxy had to tilt her head back to look up at him. She opened her mouth, but not a single protest came out. She barely kept herself from drooling with desire for him.

And so instead, Foxy flung herself at him. Like always, she leaped before she looked and nearly toppled off the bed. Like always, Joe caught her securely in his arms.

For the second time in their lives, Foxy's lips met his. That first kiss had been chaste in comparison. This kiss was a blazing inferno.

Sensations and emotions flooded Foxy. Warmth. Desire. Fire. Need. Satiation.

This was it.

He was it.

It was Joe.

Joe was the one.

She'd found her soulmate. She was wrapped up

in his arms, experiencing pure bliss as Joe deepened their kiss. Not a single one of her visions, or gut feelings, or even her imagination, could possibly compare to being embraced and ravished by Joe Matthews.

Gone was the quiet boy with a calculating mind. Here and present was a grown man with a raging appetite, and it was for her. Foxy hungered right back for him. But her stomach felt settled. Everything in her felt right and whole and perfect.

A voice cleared from the doorway. That was what finally broke them apart. With Foxy still wrapped inside his arms, she and Joe looked up to see the farmer and his wife standing in the doorway.

"Brother and sister, huh?"

Joe and Foxy looked at one another. What she felt for this man was beyond sibling affection. Still, a cold shiver replaced the warmth that had overcome her in Joe's arms. Foxy pulled back when she got a bead on the sensation.

"Daria! We have to get to Daria."

CHAPTER THIRTEEN

Joe took the turn slowly. He mainly used his left hand to make the left-handed turn. His right hand was currently and irrevocably preoccupied, locked in gear with Foxy's left hand.

After thanking the bewildered farm couple whose gazes were fixed on Joe and Foxy's joined hands, the newly minted soulmates had made their way out of the house and to Joe's towed car in the drive. Joe had held onto Foxy's hand down the stairs, out the front door, and to the passenger seat. He reluctantly released her hand to climb into the driver's side, then he scooped her fingers back into his and reclaimed his woman. He wasn't looking forward to putting the car in park as they pulled up to the state foster home, but it had to be done.

Turning off the ignition, Joe bent his head and pressed a kiss to each of Foxy's knuckles. She grinned down at him, eyes shining brightly. Joe could've sworn he was looking into a supernova as her gaze focused solely on him. He never dreamed he could be this happy, feel this content. All that could make this moment better was another kiss from the woman he had loved for as long as he'd known what the word meant.

And then he realized he now had that right.

Joe leaned over the console. Foxy met him more than halfway. Their kiss was an actual supernova.

Gravity pushed in on him, causing Joe to fall deeper into Foxy's touch. He felt as though his world were expanding and collapsing at the same time. While stars and galaxies died and were reborn around him, Joe reached for the bright light that was Foxy. He kissed her until he was senseless, only coming up when the oxygen finally ran out.

"I can't believe it was you all along," she said after she gasped in not one but two lungfuls of air.

"I didn't need any extrasensory powers to tell me you are an amazing woman," he said once he caught his breath. "I knew the first moment I met you."

"The first moment you met me, you stuck your tongue out at me and made a face."

"I was seven," Joe protested. "I thought girls were gross. But you were the first person I warmed up to."

Foxy ran her fingers along his temple and down to his chin, tracing the contours of his face. With each touch, Joe felt like he was being reborn into a new man. A stronger version of himself.

"Now," Joe said after another quick peck, "let's go in and check on this kid."

"Her name's Daria. You'll love her. She wants to be a superhero when she grows up, right all the injustices of the world. Like someone else I know."

Joe had never had a vivid imagination as a kid. He'd just had an innate sense of when something was wrong. When he saw it, he had the urge to right it.

Looking up at the state foster home, he got that inkling that something was wrong. Walking in through the doors, he was hit with a pungent smell of unclean. Bright Horizons had been an old structure, but each care worker that had been in charge had kept it neat and tidy.

Walking down the halls, the children looked unclean. Not filthy. Just not cared for. At Bright

Horizons, daily baths or showers were nonnegotiable. Many of these children looked as though they had gone a whole week without getting any parts of their bodies under a running faucet.

They flinched as Joe and Foxy came near them. None would hold their eye contact for longer than a second. In the distance, Joe could hear the muffled sounds of crying.

Foxy's fingers tightened their hold on his. Joe pulled her tightly to him. Foster care had been hard on both of them, but neither of them had suffered serious abuse. The signs were here that this place was darker than Bright Horizons.

Being brought up in the foster system after both of his parents died, and his maternal grandparents turned over their rights to him, had been a large part of the reason why Joe went into the law. He'd hated that, as a kid, he didn't have the power to speak up for himself. He had to rely on adults, and that wasn't something that came naturally to kids that had been abandoned. It wasn't until he had his law degree in his hand that Joe finally felt a real shift in power. Looking at these kids, he was reminded of the powerlessness he'd run from all those years ago.

As District Attorney, he would have the power to do something about this situation. As D.A., who would be the legal representative for the Department of Family Services. He could make a change that would improve these kids' lives.

Joe ached to tell the forlorn kids he passed this. He wanted them to lift their chins and know that change was on its way once he was in power. He would use his power to make their lives better.

A door at the end of the hall opened. A tall man who looked like he'd been a linebacker a lifetime ago walked out first. He was followed by a gray-haired woman who brought to mind a scarecrow with her black hair and perpetually narrowed gaze. Actually, on second glance, Joe realized the woman's hair was a pattern of black and a gray so pale it could almost pass as white.

"Thank you for coming, Commissioner Benson," said the scarecrow of a woman.

Benson? Why did Joe know that name? The man in question looked up, and recognition dawned in both men's eyes.

Rich had shown Joe a picture of this man at some point over the last week. This was Roger Benson. Benson sat on the Board of Commissioners, who would appoint the new D.A. to fill the vacant seat.

"Captain Matthews?"

Commissioner Benson looked Joe up and down

twice. When the man's shrewd gaze came back to Joe's a second time, Joe was certain he saw disapproval in his gaze.

"I thought we weren't meeting until tomorrow." Commissioner Benson straightened his tie as he took a step closer to shake Joe's hand. "I see you're eager."

Joe let go of Foxy's hand and held out his to shake the commissioner's. "I didn't realize you were here, sir. It's a happy coincidence. I'm here on family business."

"Family?" Commissioner Benson looked at Foxy. "This is your sister?"

"No, Foxy is my…"

"I'm his soulmate." Foxy supplied when Joe's silence went on a beat too long.

Soulmate hadn't been the qualifier Joe had planned to use. Girlfriend seemed childish. Fiancée wasn't accurate as he hadn't asked. Soulmate was accurate but not necessarily the best description for the serious man who stood gaping at the two of them.

Commissioner Benson dropped Joe's hand. Foxy promptly picked it up and laced her fingers with his.

"Soulmate?" said Benson. "And you say your name is Foxy?"

Foxy nodded. "Foxy Morningstar James."

"Foxy works with another foster home," Joe interjected before she could add any more details. "She's working on her Elevated Care Certification as part of her job at the Bright Horizons Foster Home."

"Commendable," said Commissioner Benson, his disapproving features relaxing slightly.

"I'm also clairsentient," Foxy offered. "We're here because I felt that one of the kids in this home was in distress."

Commissioner Benson's gaze went back to Joe. For his part, Joe gave the man a weak smile, wondering if his dream job was right now slipping through his fingers. One thing Joe did not let go of was his soulmate's hand. He'd waited too long to win that particular reward. Whatever the future threw at him, or withheld from him, he would do it with this woman at his side.

"Ms. Foxy, you came to rescue me."

A skinny bundle of arms and legs and tangled hair flew against Foxy's middle. Even though Daria was slight, the little girl nearly knocked Foxy over with her embrace. Foxy squeezed the child back tightly, feeling worried that she mostly felt skin and bones.

When Daria had first come to Bright Horizons, she refused any kind of touch. It was common amongst foster kids. Those children had been abandoned by the first people who were meant to love them unconditionally. So it was no wonder that they had trouble accepting affection from strangers.

"This place is full of villains," Daria whispered in Foxy's ear.

Though Daria's idea of a whisper was loud enough for those at the back of a movie theater to hear her. They were standing in a common room with a few other foster kids. Most of them looked over at Foxy and Daria, sending Daria derisive looks.

Foxy knew those looks well. Before she and her sisters had come to stay at Bright Horizons, they'd been in a few unsavory places where kids and adults preyed on the vulnerable. But she'd been a James.

With one James, you used caution. With two, you ran. All three of them together had climbed to the top of the food chain of every foster home they'd been dropped in. And now, they ran what had once been one of the more notorious homes in the state.

Not only were they running Bright Horizons now, but they'd uprooted it and settled the establishment into new digs on a ranch. Daria was one of theirs. She was here at the State Home temporarily until they got her back. Part of the deal with them getting her back was Foxy earning her Elevated Care certification.

The State believed Daria was special needs due to a little misunderstanding. The little girl may have believed she was a superhero. There may have been a stack of medical records of bruises and sprains and broken limbs at the ER. And maybe a representative from the state witnessed the child leaping onto a horse because she believed it was magical and would help her flee being taken by the state.

Yeah, just a bunch of misunderstandings. Joe was helping file the paperwork for Savy and Charlie to adopt Daria's older brother Denny. Once that ink dried, and Foxy had her Elevated Care certification, there should be no reason that they couldn't get Daria back home with them where she belonged.

But first, Daria had to survive this State Home. Unlike the James girls, Daria was here all by herself. Neither did she have her brother looking after her. Worse than that, the little superhero was without her cape.

Without the cape covering her pale flesh, Foxy saw that there were a few more bruises on her arms and legs. They could've been from Daria's superhero antics. But Foxy somehow doubted it. The cold feeling increased in the pit of Foxy's stomach.

"Did someone hurt you, Daria?" Foxy held the little girl's bruised arms gingerly.

"Oh, this? I got this from spying on Ms. Monroe."

"You were spying on the head care provider here?"

Daria nodded. "Have you seen her? She looks like Cruella Deville, but without the polka dots."

Foxy couldn't deny the comparison. Ms. Monroe had a stern, shrewd look about her. And her black hair had uniform white streaks that couldn't have come from a dye job. That hairstyle looked like something from the supernatural.

"Ms. Benson looks like a villain. But also," Daria leaned in close to give Foxy another one of her stage whispers. "She's never tried to hug me like you and Ms. Savy. None of these kids have ever been hugged. I asked. They don't even do chores here."

That was a complaint after Savy's heart. But which one of Daria's statements would Savy love more? To know that Daria not only missed hugs, but she missed doing chores.

"That's how I knew there was something off about this place," Daria continued. Her voice was now low enough to be an actual whisper. "So I crawled through the air vents."

Foxy seized her thin shoulders. "You crawled through the air vents. Daria, that's dangerous."

"I was careful. No one saw me."

Foxy gentled her hold. Daria really required twenty-four-seven supervision. Not because she was a troubled youth. Because trouble attached to her like the smudges of dirt on her chin.

"This morning, Ms. Monroe and that creepy guy were in the office."

Creepy guy? She must mean Commissioner Benson. Foxy had gotten creep factor from him too, but she'd held her tongue. The man had something to do with Joe getting appointed as District Attorney. In fact, Joe was talking to him right now.

Foxy didn't know much about politics. She knew that a commissioner was some kind of politician. She supposed she'd have to deal with the likes of them if she was going to be a politician's wife.

Huh, look at that. Foxy James never thought she'd be anywhere near politics. But if that's what Joe wanted, then she would make compromises. She was serious when she said the world needed a good man like Joe. She'd just have to be the woman at his side protecting him from the evils of politics and power-hungry politicians. It would seem that that crusade might have to start with Commissioner Benson.

"They're making kids sick," said Daria.

"What do you mean?"

"They're making them mental on purpose."

"Daria, that is inappropriate language. People

with mental disabilities need our compassion and understanding."

"But they're doing it on purpose, Ms. Foxy. I heard them say it. They're trying to make me mentally disabled too."

Tears welled in Daria's eyes. She didn't even try to fight them. They spilled down her cheeks, leaving tracks through the smudges of grime.

Foxy pulled the girl to her and held her tight. "I know this is hard, sweetheart. We're going to get you out of here soon. I promise."

"I want to go home now. I don't want to be mentally disabilitied."

Foxy took a deep breath. She stared at Daria. She knew this was an unfounded fear. But for some reason, the cold dread that had first brought her here wouldn't leave her belly. Not even now that she'd seen that Daria was somewhat healthy and mostly whole.

Something was still wrong.

CHAPTER FIFTEEN

"As you can see, we are all up to code here." Ms. Monroe's kitten heels clacked on the linoleum as she strode down the hall.

The sound reminded Joe of gunfire. However, instead of felling any of the bad guys on the opposite side, every kid in the vicinity of the sound jerked to attention while also flinching away and disappearing around a corner or into a nook or behind a door.

Joe peeked into the room that Ms. Monroe indicated. Inside, things were a little untidy. The floors were sticky and squeaky under his shoes. And there was still that ever-present smell of something unwashed.

It didn't cling to Ms. Monroe. She was dressed

impeccably in a pristine blouse and a skirt that rivaled what Charlotte O'Dell had been wearing the other day. Her nails were polished to perfection. Her eye makeup expertly applied. It didn't make her look pretty. It made her look severe and intimidating.

The foster kids in the room shuffled about under her scrutiny. All conversation stopped the moment Ms. Monroe darkened the doorway. Every little body went as still as a cockroach, holding its position on a wall, hoping that as long as it didn't move, it wouldn't be noticed by the predator.

For his part, Commissioner Benson's gaze kept flitting back to his watch as though there was someplace else he'd rather be. He did not cross the threshold with Joe and Ms. Monroe. Neither did he lean on the doorjamb. His upturned nose wrinkled as though he smelled the unwashed scent as well and was doing everything in his power to make sure none of it touched his person.

Joe took in the room of silent kids. A few of them snuck glances back at him, but no one said a word. Foxy's voice sounded in Joe's head that something wasn't right with the place. He couldn't disagree with her. But neither could he find any evidence that something was out of place.

"When I was in foster care, it was never this quiet," said Joe.

"That's because they didn't have good drugs when you were a kid."

Joe blinked once, then twice. He looked over to Ms. Monroe, hoping to hear a jesting laugh or see a joking smile. The black and white-haired woman looked as serious as ever.

"A number of these children have major issues," Ms. Monroe went on to say. "Everything from panic attacks, PTSD, anxiety, and depression, along with physical disabilities."

A lot of children in the foster system had some form of PTSD. It could be a result of being born addicted by what their parents put into their own veins. Or it could be trauma that came postnatal. These kids weren't born with the same deck as others, which is why they so desperately needed advocates.

"I understand you came from the foster system yourself, Captain Matthews?"

Joe nodded. "My father was killed in Iraq not long after I was born. My mother's parents wanted her to give me up for adoption because I was biracial."

One of the kids looked up at this admission. The

kid didn't look biracial, but it was hard to tell just by looking at anyone what their cultural make up was. Joe had always hated when someone asked him *what are you*. The kid wasn't looking at Joe's skin color trying to place his ethnicity. He stole a glance directly into Joe's eyes as though to ask *who* was he.

"It looks like you've made something of yourself," said Commissioner Benson, finally joining in on the conversation but not stepping over the threshold and into the room. "Law degree, JAG officer, and now a candidate for District Attorney. You're an example to these kids."

Joe nodded, his gaze still holding the kid, who was silently eyeing him. "I was fostered at a home and then adopted by wonderful people. Then I used the VA benefits from my father to pay for college."

"VA benefits?" said the kid, rising from his place on the worn sofa. "What's that?"

"Justin." Ms. Monroe's voice was like a whip cracking across the room. "We only speak if spoken to."

Justin pursed his lips. There was a quiver about his lower lip as though he desperately wanted to speak.

"It's fine," said Joe. "I'm happy to explain. VA benefits means Veteran Benefits. They're monies provided for any surviving member of a military person."

"My mom was a soldier," said Justin. "They say she fell and died."

This kid's mother was a fallen soldier. That meant she'd died in the line of combat, not that she'd necessarily fallen down.

"Do you think I'd have something like that? I want to go to college, too."

"Of course you do," said Joe, stepping forward. "I could—"

"Justin, Captain Matthews is busy," Ms. Monroe cut Joe off physically by stepping in front of him, as well as with her terse words. "This is something we can discuss later."

She turned with a perfect about-face that made Joe wonder if she was also a product of the military. Maybe the daughter of a drill sergeant, if she wasn't one herself.

Ms. Monroe marched Joe out the door, shutting it behind her. "I'm sorry about that," she said.

"No, I don't mind at all. I'd be happy to talk more to him or any other kid about military benefits and how to use them to pay for college or anything else."

"Like I said, most of these kids have disabilities

that would preclude them from succeeding at college, let alone getting acceptance."

Joe wanted to protest that. A disability didn't preclude anyone from higher education. Soldiers who served their country came back daily with wounds gotten in the line of duty. Every day, they continued to give more, even in their wounded capacity. Before Joe could raise his voice, Commissioner Benson chimed in.

"What this place needs," said Commissioner Benson, "is more funding. It's expensive to take care of all these kids. It taxes the county and state budget."

"I agree," said Joe. "And if I become DA, foster care and funding will be one of my top priorities."

Commissioner Benson grinned at that. Something in the man's grin brought to mind a snake slithering up the path. "I think you would make a good DA. You'd certainly have my vote…"

Any thought of hissing left Joe's mind at those words. He'd done it. He'd won Commissioner Benson over. And it hadn't taken a fake engagement to do so. It had just taken Joe speaking from his heart about one of his passion projects; the care of foster kids.

"It's just that… soulmate of yours…I don't know if she's D.A. wife material."

Joe's shoulders caved at Commissioner Benson's words. But his heart refused to sink. It was too buoyed by Foxy's returned affection. It looked like he was back to square one because there was no way he would throw over his soulmate for his dream job.

"You're right," Joe admitted. "Foxy definitely isn't D.A. wife material. But she cares about these kids as much as I do. Likely more because she wants to work with the ones who are most troubled as an Elevated Care Provider. With her by my side, she'll help me in my crusade to ensure foster homes get the funding and staffing they need to take care of these kids."

Joe's heart pounded in his chest. He wasn't sure if it was for the loss of his dream job or if it was the adrenaline of standing up for his dream girl. As he looked at Commissioner Benson and Ms. Monroe, he witnessed a silent communication take place between the two of them.

Finally, Commissioner Benson turned back to Joe. He held out his hand. "I think I believe you. And I think you'll be the perfect man for the job."

CHAPTER SIXTEEN

Once the car door shut and they were enclosed in the car, Foxy and Joe reached for each other's hands. Foxy wasn't sure if Joe reached first or if she did. Foxy entwined the fingers of her left hand with Joe's right one. Joe pressed the palm of his left hand until it was flush with Foxy's right one.

They held onto each other tight. Both clearly needing the contact. Was it being in a less than savory foster home that had ignited the need? Was it the sparks of new love that still burned bright around them? Did it matter?

Foxy turned to Joe. He was already gazing down at her. His face was so familiar, so dear to her. Joe looked at her like she was a buried treasure he'd just unearthed. Had he always looked at her like that?

How had she missed these clear signs of adoration? How had she not realized that this was the man she was meant to spend the rest of her life with?

"It's pretty much a done deal," Joe said.

"Yes, I suppose it is."

Gone was the comforting security that always surrounded her in Joe's presence. In its place was a raging desire that Foxy wasn't entirely sure what to do with. She wanted to kiss him. She wanted to hold him close. She wanted him to feel just how fast he made her heart beat.

"We'll announce it next week," said Joe.

Announce it? He hadn't even asked her to marry him yet. They hadn't even gone on a single date.

Though did that matter? This was more than a done deal. It was the real deal. They were each other's soulmate.

No man had ever been as close to her as Joe. No man had her trust the way he did. No man had her heart

"Rich will be thrilled," Joe said as he rubbed his thumb across her knuckles.

"Rich? Your campaign manager? I didn't get the sense he liked me very much."

"No." Joe barked a laugh. "He thought you'd be a liability to my campaign."

"A liability?"

"Now it doesn't matter because Commissioner Benson just gave me his blessing."

"Benson? The creepy old guy blessed our engagement?"

Joe blinked, and when he did, a little of the haze of desire cleared from his eyes. "Engagement?"

The clarity in Joe's gaze confused Foxy. "Joe, what done-deal-blessing are you talking about?"

"My appointment as District Attorney. Commissioner Benson was the last hold out. After meeting me today, he gave me his endorsement."

"Oh." Foxy let her fingers unfurl from his.

Joe did not let her go. Instead, he held tight and quirked an eyebrow. "Engagement?"

"It was a misunderstanding." Foxy tried again to pull her hand away.

Joe would not let her go. Joe took both of her hands, turning them until his palms were on the back of her hands. Then he pressed both of Foxy's palms to his chest, right where his heart beat.

"I understand it perfectly well," he said. "I am going to marry you."

Tears pricked Foxy's eyes. She closed her lids, but that didn't hold them at bay. "Even if I could be a liability to your career?"

Joe pressed his hands into Foxy's until her fingers jumped with every beat of his pounding heart. "This is yours. Has been since we were kids. It won't beat without you. The true liability, the only danger to my life, is not having you in it."

Foxy let out a long sigh, not realizing until then that she had been holding her breath. Joe caught the tear that slipped out of one eye. Before the next tear could fall, his lips were at her temple. He caught that tear and the others that fell. Then his mouth was on hers. Foxy should've tasted the salt of her tears. It was sweet warmth that filled her mouth as Joe ran his lips across hers.

When Joe pulled away, Foxy was floating. She hadn't known that such happiness was even possible. So why was her gut still tightening with dread?

Looking out the passenger side window, Foxy saw a small figure standing in the doorway of the state home. Daria's lip trembled as she looked at the two of them. Then a hand snaked out, and Ms. Monroe pulled the child inside and shut the door.

"I'm sorry we can't take her with us yet," said Joe. "You saw that she's okay."

Daria was physically okay. The adoption paperwork was moving forward. She would be back at the ranch soon.

All of those facts did not negate what Foxy felt. The cold twisting was still there. Though muted.

"She thinks they're trying to make her sick," said Foxy.

"She thinks someone is trying to poison her?"

"No. She thinks they're trying to make her crazy. She said she heard the Commissioner and Ms. Monroe talking about disabilities."

"Yeah, Ms. Monroe said many of the kids there have physical and mental disabilities."

"Daria said they were trying to give her one."

"She's what? Seven? I'm sure she misunderstood. In fact, they're working to bring in more funding for the kids to help them with their issues."

Foxy knew he was right. It was the logical explanation. No one could make a kid have a disability.

"Still," she said, "something felt off about that place."

"It's not a perfect place, but everything is run to the letter of the law. I think with more funding, they could make it more comfortable for the kids."

That sounded good. But the feeling still nagged at her.

"Fox, you can't always rely on your feelings. You yourself once said you have a fifty-fifty accuracy."

"Not about danger. Are you sure there wasn't anything weird about Commissioner Benson?"

"Foxy, you can't go around disparaging people based on the gas in your stomach."

Her stomach went numb at Joe's words. Her fingers clenched into fists at his chest.

"Don't do that. Don't pull away." Joe held her hands tight. He bowed his head and sighed before speaking again. "I'm sorry. That was wrong of me to say it like that. I believe you. I believe in you. But, sweetheart, we can't chase down every sensation you have, especially when lives are on the line. I can make a difference as D.A. I will make a difference, but I gotta get the job first."

Foxy knew Joe would make a difference. He always did the right thing. Joe would never rest when something was wrong. He'd come with her and investigated, and they'd found nothing wrong. This had to be one of those times when her gut was wrong.

Joe kissed her knuckles before he gave them

back to her. Then he kissed her forehead before making sure she was buckled in tight. When he started the car, Foxy settled back in the seat and decidedly ignored the nagging in her belly.

oe settled his shoulders back into the driver's seat. He shifted his form, turning his body so that he could gaze down at Foxy. She wasn't asleep, as he'd suspected. She sat still in the passenger seat, eyes out the front window, staring at nothing. She was quiet like she'd been for the last twenty minutes on the ride home.

They were parked in the drive of the Flying Cross Ranch now. Their hands were still entwined. He knew they couldn't sit here all day, even though he wanted to. The last thing he wanted to do was let go of Foxy's hand.

It had taken too long to gain a hold of her hand, of her heart. The cold words he'd said to her before departing from the State Home still hung in the air between them.

If he let her go now, what if she wouldn't reach for him again after this? She held his fingers tightly now. Her fingers pressed into his, down to the webbing. Joe returned the caress, wanting desperately to remain a part of her.

"Foxy..."

Joe's words were lost when she turned to face him. His breath caught in his throat as those bright eyes lit upon him. The gold flecks that had always been ever-present in her hazel gaze were dim.

Had he done that? Had his words cut her so deeply that he'd dulled her shine. If having his career dream meant pulling a shadow over his dream woman, there would be no contest.

"Fox, I'm sorry."

"I know." Foxy curled her fingers over his. She brought Joe's hand to her lips and kissed the back of his flesh softly. "You have to get ready for this evening."

That had not been what Joe was about to say. It was true that he had to get ready for this evening. To get ready for the announcement that he was throwing his hat in the ring to become District Attorney.

But was the announcement even necessary when he now had a nod from every commissioner on the board? Joe didn't want to go to a party to talk to people. He wanted to stay in the car, in this little cocoon that he and Foxy had made.

"You were right," Foxy said. "Once you get this position of power, you'll be able to do more for those kids, for the whole community, than anyone else. You are the perfect man for this job, Joe. And I am so proud of you."

There was the spark back in her eyes. The golden flecks flashed at him, warming Joe from the outside in. He pulled her to him, tucking her face into his neck, pulling her chest flush against his until he felt her heartbeat sync with his.

"You'll be with me?" he asked.

"Are you sure you want me there?" she said. "Maybe we should keep our relationship quiet until after you secure the position."

Joe pulled back to look down into her face. There, he found what he feared. Foxy was serious.

"We're a packaged deal, Foxy. They can't have me without you."

Foxy traced Joe's bottom lip with her index finger. "Then I'll try to be quiet. Not talk about any of my gut feelings if I get any."

Joe opened his mouth to refute that. But he promptly pressed his lips together to hold back any sentiment. It would be better if she didn't say anything tonight. Just for tonight. Just to these people. They would figure out the rest as it came.

Lifting their joined hands, Joe pressed his lips to Foxy's knuckles. He kissed each one in turn. When she pulled away to get out of the car, he let her go.

Joe watched Foxy walk away from him. He sat, tracing her every step until she was behind the door of the guest house. Finally, he climbed out of the car.

"So, that finally happened."

Joe looked over to see his father leaning against the front porch. Haran Matthews held a glass of pale brown liquid in one hand. Condensation ran down the sides of his fingers as he sipped his tea in the afternoon sun.

"You knew?" said Joe.

"Everyone knew," said Father Matthews. "Except, of course, Foxy."

The two Matthews men looked to the guest house. From this distance, Joe saw Foxy's shadow move across the curtained window. He hated this short distance between them and wanted to go to her. To bring her back into his embrace. To kiss her lush mouth. Or simply to hold her hand again.

"The two of you are not sleeping there together before vows are said."

"Yes, sir." Joe sighed. Then he let out a chuckle. "I did it, dad. District Attorney is mine."

Father Matthews tilted his head and regarded his son. He sat his empty tea glass on the railing and opened his arms. Joe felt like a schoolboy as he went into his father's embrace.

"I'm proud of you, my boy. You worked hard, and all of your dreams are coming true." Father Matthews pulled back to regard his son. "So, why don't you look happy?"

"I am," said Joe. "It's just... I met this kid at the state home. He could've been me if I didn't have you. Lost his parents to the war in Iraq. He wants to go to school but doesn't have the means."

"If his parents were in the service, then he should qualify for the GI Bill?"

"He didn't even know about it. I want to get a program going to make sure the kids in foster care know about their benefits."

"He should have survivor's benefits now to help him along."

"I don't think he knew about them either."

"The staff at the home would know," said Father

Matthews. "Though your mother and I had to fight to get yours."

"You had to fight Bright Horizons to get my benefits?"

"No, your maternal grandparents. They tried to keep what your birth mother left you for themselves. They were pocketing your benefits from both your father and your mother while you were in foster care."

"You never told me that."

"You were a kid. As your guardian, I did what was necessary to take care of you and make sure you had the best shot at life."

Joe gripped his father's shoulder. If it weren't for this man, he had no idea what his life would've turned into. "I wish there were more like you, Dad."

"There are," said his father. "Those James girls are going to save the world, one foster child at a time."

Joe followed his father's gaze to the east side of the ranch. Savy was in the garden with the four foster kids currently in her care. She threw her head back and laughed at something one of the kids said. The children, even the sour-looking one named Denny, all laughed and grinned. Those kids were the lucky ones. They couldn't find anyone better to care for them, to fight for their futures than Savy and Foxy James.

"Before I forget," Father Matthews pulled an envelope from inside the door to the big house. "This came for Foxy while you were away."

The envelope read that it was from the law offices of Charlotte O'Dell. "What is this?"

"I believe it's a letter of recommendation from the family law practitioner that helped Foxy a couple of years ago. It was Ms. O'Dell's father that helped us when we fought your grandparents for your benefits. It's my understanding that Ms. O'Dell is still fighting for foster kids and getting their benefits from the state."

"From the state?"

Joe thought back to his lunch date the other day with Charlotte. She had said something about getting benefits from the government. Joe hadn't thought much of it, until now. A light wind blew, prickling the hair at the nape of Joe's neck. A roiling began in his belly. It grumbled like he was hungry. But food was the last thing on Joe's mind. A cold feeling settled in his gut, a feeling that he couldn't ignore.

CHAPTER EIGHTEEN

The shower didn't do Foxy the good she needed. It washed away the dirt and grime of the last two days, but it didn't make the gnawing feeling in her stomach go away.

Something was off.

Foxy took a deep breath and let it out slowly. Then another and another. Slowly, the cold, twisting feeling began to recede. What took its place was the warm, soothing love she felt for Joe.

That love had always been there. Foxy just hadn't taken the time to examine it. She'd always been so preoccupied with what was going on in other people's lives that she had nearly missed out on the love of her life.

That way of thinking, that way of feeling, was

done. From now on, Foxy was going to keep her nose—and her belly—out of other people's business and focus on her own life. She was going to be the wife of the District Attorney. Those would be big shoes to fill. Likely high heels, which were not her favorite.

She'd had to wear them when she'd performed with her mother and her sisters. Foxy preferred flats and sneakers so that she was grounded. The stems had taken her body too high from the earth and its natural vibrations.

She'd wear heels for Joe. He was her soulmate. She would be everything he needed her to be. And that was not a woman who walked in flats and was led around by her bellyaching.

Foxy turned her head toward the door. But at the last minute, she closed her mouth and looked the other way. The door opened, and Savy came in.

"What?" said Savy. "You didn't hear me coming?"

"Hey, sis."

"The van is back, and it's had a tune-up. Thanks for that."

"That's great." Though it hadn't been Foxy. It had likely been Joe that had made that call. Like when they were kids, he was watching out for her and anticipating her needs.

"So, you and Joe spent the night together." Savy plopped down on the sofa and waggled her eyes up at her sister. "How did that go?"

A slow smile spread across Foxy's face at the thought of waking up in Joe's arms. And then there was that first kiss. Well, actually, the second kiss. Soon, she would be waking up like that every morning for the rest of her life.

"No way," said Savy. "He finally made his move?"

"What do you mean, he *finally* made his move? Did you know about the kiss?"

"He kissed you last night?"

"Not that kiss. The one from ten years ago?"

"Ten years ago? Do you mean when you were fourteen? I'll kill him."

"You will not. You and Charlie were getting up to the same thing at that age."

"The two of you are not staying in this guest house together without vows being exchanged."

Foxy rolled her eyes. Then she flew into her sister's arms. "It's him, Sav. He's the one. He's the man I've been dreaming about all these years. Only it wasn't a dream. It was a memory. I forgot all about it. What kind of psychic does that make me?"

"You're not a psychic."

"No, it's even worse." Foxy wrung her hands as

she paced the length of the room. "All my life, I've had all these feelings. And now I've come to realize that I don't even know what they mean half the time. How could I have missed him when he was standing right in front of me for so long? He even kissed me, and I didn't see it."

"You have him now." Savy stood and stopped her sister, bringing her into a hug. "And he has you. That's what matters."

"Yeah." Foxy sniffled into her big sister's shoulder. "Yeah, I do, and I'm gonna focus with my eyes instead of my stomach."

"What?" asked Savy, pulling away.

Instead of answering her sister, Foxy turned to the door a second before the knock sounded. It had to be him. It had to be Joe.

Maybe he'd come for another kiss. Maybe he'd come just to be near her. It didn't matter why he'd come. Foxy simply wanted to be in his presence. But when she opened the door, it wasn't Joe.

"Is she okay?" asked Denny.

"Yes, Denny. Daria is fine. Impatient, up to her old superhero tricks and spying, but she's not hurting."

"You said you got a feeling," said Denny. The anxiety in the boy's voice was palpable.

Foxy bit her lip. She hated that her gut had caused this kid to worry. "I did. But she's okay. She'll be home with us soon. I'm sure of it."

"Because you got another feeling?" Denny's tone was biting, accusatory.

"That's enough, Denny," said Savy. "Go finish your chores."

Denny scowled at them both as he took off down the steps of the guest house. The fluttering in Foxy's belly turned back to angry bees. She took a deep breath. And then another. The sensation wouldn't stop this time.

She thought of Joe. Pulling up an image of his strong, certain face. But the vision was hazy.

"Denny's right," said Foxy. "I have to help Daria. And the only way I can do that is to get the right credentials."

"I thought you said you got the two letters," said Savy.

"I had. But I kinda stole the man of the woman who agreed to write the second recommendation letter. When she finds out, I doubt she'll have anything favorable to say about me."

"Where are you going?"

"Into town to get another letter of recommendation."

Foxy grabbed the keys to the van and left the guest house. The drive into town was a blur. Her mind was far too focused on settling the nagging in her gut. But the more she hushed it, the louder it grew in her mind.

Pulling into the parking lot of Ramos's Deli and Cafe, Foxy put the van in park and hopped out. The roiling in her stomach was feeling more like a belly ache than any clairsentient feeling she'd ever gotten before. This was the only way she knew to solve the problem with Daria.

She was going to march into the restaurant and get Travis to write her a letter of recommendation. The parking lot was near to full. It hadn't been that way a couple of years ago before she worked here. Foot traffic had increased at Ramos's when she worked there and gave out unsolicited advice and predictions. Customers may have come for the spectacle of the psychic waitress, but they stayed for the food. Travis owed some of his success to her, and she wasn't leaving without that letter.

Foxy marched up to the door of the restaurant. But something nagged her, causing her to pause. A light wind blew over her shoulders, causing the hair at the nape of her neck to prickle. She glanced over to the left and what she saw stopped her heart.

Joe stood at the door of Charlotte O'Dell's law offices. Charlotte stood in the doorway, a huge flirtatious smile on her face. She leaned in and kissed Joe on the cheek. He did not pull away. He followed her into the office as she beckoned him inside.

The whole scene left Foxy feeling cold and numb. She had not seen that one coming.

CHAPTER NINETEEN

"Thank you for seeing me, Ms. O'Dell."

"Ms. O'Dell? I think if we're seeing each other, Captain Matthews, then it should be on a first-name basis." Charlotte pressed her palm to Joe's chest and came in to kiss him on his cheek. When he flinched at her touch, her smile sank, and she stepped back. "Unless we're no longer seeing each other."

Joe took a deep inhale. He let the breath out with an apology. "I'm sorry, Charlotte."

Charlotte beckoned him into the building. Joe followed, girding his loins for what was to come. He hated breakups, which is why he had avoided dating for much of his adult life. No matter how perfect the woman was for him, she could never be Foxy.

"Tell me what I did wrong?" said Charlotte once they were in her office with the door shut. "Is it my high-powered job? Is it the six-inch heels? I'm always taller than the men I date, but my high arches can't stand flats. You still have a good inch on me with my stilettos on."

"Charlotte." Joe held up his hand to stop her diatribe. "It's none of those things. You're great. You're perfect."

"Logically, I can't be perfect if you're dumping me."

"It's not you. It's me."

Charlotte balked at that.

"Actually, it's someone else."

"You're not making any sense, Captain Matthews."

"I was already in love with another woman before I even met you."

"And let me guess, she realized what she was missing when you started dating me?"

"No, she didn't even remember that there was anything between us. She actually encouraged me to date you. Until she had a vision of our first kiss as kids and then realized that I was her soulmate and—"

"This has to be the most nonsensical conversation I've ever had in my life," said Charlotte.

She looked at Joe as though he were crazy. Because the words coming out of his mouth were crazy. Had he have been talking to Foxy, the words would've made complete sense. That thought made Joe grin.

"No, I take that back," said Charlotte. "I've had crazier conversations with your friend, Foxy."

The despair of being dumped dissipated from Charlotte's face and was replaced by suspicion. Joe quickly changed the subject before the lawyer's deductive reason focused too pointedly on Foxy.

"Never mind," said Joe. "That's not why I'm here."

"So, you're breaking up with me and also here to ask for something else?"

"It's work-related. You practice family law. You help foster kids. Can I ask what the nature of your work is with the kids?"

"You know I can't break client-attorney privilege." Charlotte crossed her arms over her chest. It was a move Joe pulled many a time. She was in full counselor mode now.

"I'm not asking you to reveal anything that isn't public record. I'm just not sure what I'm looking for. I was at the state foster home earlier and something one of the kids said just won't leave me alone."

Charlotte uncrossed her arms and leaned a little forward. "What did they say?"

"Well, it's what they didn't know. He was a soldier's kid. But he didn't know he had access to the GI bill being the survivor of military personnel. And when I tried to give him more information, the caretaker steered me out of the room."

"I see." Charlotte leaned back in her seat, but she didn't cross her arms over her chest to ward him off. She tapped her index finger on her lower lip and regarded him.

"You see?" said Joe. "You see what?"

Charlotte continued to tap her lower lip as she regarded him. Just a moment ago, she had looked up at him with the trust that came with believing they were going to be life partners. Now she looked at him as though he was an adversary.

"Charlotte, I want to help these kids. If there's anything you know that could help me help them, please…"

"You'll want to look into The Marshall Project."

"What will that case tell me?"

"It's not a case. It's a nationwide investigation."

"An investigation of what?"

"I think you suspect what it is."

Joe pursed his lips. He tapped his index finger on

the wooden arm of the chair he sat in. He did not want to voice what was formulating in his mind about what was happening back at that state home. When Charlotte voiced it for him, it was no better.

"You know there are bad foster parents who pocket kids' benefits."

Joe nodded. His own maternal grandparents had done that to him. "But this kid doesn't have any other family, as far as I know."

Charlotte remained mute again, waiting for him to voice what he didn't want to acknowledge.

"It's the state, isn't it?" Joe didn't need Charlotte to confirm. It all added up. Especially when he remembered Ms. Monroe hushing him about the GI Bill and survivor benefits. It was still a hard pill to swallow that a state agency would be taking money from children. "That can't be right."

"It's not illegal," said Charlotte. "It's unethical. It's downright dirty, but they're not breaking the letter of the law. They're saying it's being used to fund their care. I've even found evidence that they're looking through these kids' school and health records to see if they can be labeled as mentally disabled, so that they'll collect more money."

Mental disabilitied. That's what Foxy said Daria

had told her. Foxy had been right. Her clairsentience had uncovered a huge conspiracy.

"The Marshall Project has found at least thirty-six states where state foster care agencies are using this practice of taking kids' benefits to pay for their foster care, that includes survivor benefits, veterans' benefits, and Social Security benefits. They're raking in millions every year."

"But foster homes are funded through taxpayer dollars and federal and state grants," Joe said, his mind giving a last grasp of denial.

"They say they use the funds to pay for the children's daily expenses like shelter and food, rather than just giving them cash. My law firm is a part of a class-action lawsuit regarding this matter."

"Class-action? Who are the defendants?"

"The county and the state. This was one of the ways they were trying to get more funding for children's services. By making the kids pay for this public service."

Commissioner Benson's snakelike smile popped into Joe's head. The man had mentioned that they needed more funding. Is this how he meant to get it?

"Since you're in line to be the next District Attorney of this county, you'll be representing the state for this matter."

oxy squeezed her hands in her lap. Her fingertips felt cold. She pressed them together, rubbed them on her knee, and finally rested them on the console between the driver and passenger seat. Joe did not reach for her hand to cover it with his warmth.

"Is everything okay?" Foxy asked.

"Hmm?" Joe's gaze was out the window. His hands were at ten and two, ever the responsible driver. "Yes, of course."

"You just seem distracted."

"It's a big night. This will be a big announcement. It's going to change our lives."

He'd said *our* lives and not *my* life. That was

something. At least he was still including her in his life. Or was the *our* referring to Charlotte O'Dell.

Foxy should just come out and ask him about it. Ask him what he was doing at the woman's office today. Her stomach was in absolute knots over it. She couldn't form the words.

Joe parked the car and came around to her side to hand her out. The moment his fingers touched hers, Foxy got a jolt of warmth that coursed all through her body. The nagging feeling that had been pressing her all day fled, and all she felt was the love she'd always had for the person standing beside her. Though now it was so warm, so bright, that it burned for the man kissing her fingertips.

She'd been a fool to think anything was wrong. Clearly, Joe still loved her if he was kissing her fingertips like this. It just went to show that her gut didn't know everything.

"I'm going to have to leave you," said Joe when they entered the venue.

"What?" Foxy gripped his hand tighter. "No."

"Just for a little while. Rich will take care of you."

Foxy wanted to protest that she didn't want Rich. She didn't want anyone but Joe. But Joe was already walking off. His strides were long, sure, and purposeful. His direction would take him right onto the path of Charlotte O'Dell.

The woman looked stunning in a white dress that did wonders for her complexion. She took one step toward Joe. Her legs impossibly long in six-inch heels. Meanwhile, Foxy wobbled in her one-inch kitten heels.

"So, you're the psychic he's going to throw his career over for?"

Foxy turned to see that Rich had come up behind her. She'd barely glanced at him the first time they'd met, but she remembered him. The man had a movie star's good looks, along with a grin that might've given a shark pause.

"I'm not..." She couldn't finish that sentence. The doubt in her abilities had grown so much over the past couple of days that Foxy wasn't sure what she was any longer.

On the one hand, she knew with a certainty that she and Joe were meant to be together. On the other hand, she knew that being with him would bring challenges to his dream life. Why was her happily ever after turning into a nightmare?

"I know," Rich was saying. "You're not a psychic. You're a clair... something or other. Someone who feels things deeply. I won't hide the fact that I feel that Joe choosing you will make things difficult for him to advance in politics. If he'd stuck with Charlotte, like I said, he would have a clear path to State District Attorney in a matter of years. Maybe even a shot at President one day."

Foxy's gaze ping-ponged around the room until she found Joe. Charlotte was still beside him. They weren't arm in arm, but she was clearly introducing him to important people. Something Foxy couldn't do, not unless he wanted the best table at Ramos's Deli and Cafe. Or to get good seats at a few of the state's dive bars.

"Right now, he's only the county D.A.," Rich was saying. "So, I don't think there's much harm you can do here in your own backyard."

The dark, twisty sensation knotted inside Foxy's gut. Despite the wrenching, she had a feeling Rich was wrong about that. The sensation warmed to a near burning when someone cleared their throat behind them.

"Commissioner Benson, good to see you," said Rich, sticking out his hand for a greeting.

The commissioner ignored Rich's hand. His gaze was on Foxy. The way the older man looked at her made her feel dirty inside and out.

"I hear you're getting certified in elevated care for foster kids, Ms. James," he said.

"That's correct."

"You came to visit a little girl at the state home earlier today."

"Daria. Her name's Daria."

"Can I take it that your interest in her is because she has a history of mental health illness?"

"No, Daria's a healthy adolescent."

"Who believes she's a superhero."

"So do some adults and any Marvel or Star Wars fan."

"I'm a DC guy and a Trekkie myself," said Rich. The man's sharklike grin faded with a single glance from Commissioner Benson, whose glassy eyes brought to mind those of a killer whale.

"Ms. James," said the commissioner, turning his attention back to her. "You do understand that when children are properly diagnosed, they get the additional care they need."

"I understand that," said Foxy. "Daria should not be in state foster care. She should be with her family, who love her."

"She has no family."

"I'm her family."

"Oh, it makes sense now." Commissioner Benson

flashed her those sharp white teeth. "You think you're psychic. The kid thinks she can fly. Clearly, you both have mental health issues."

Foxy opened her mouth to take this man to task. Then she promptly shut it. In hindsight, she'd like to say that her discretion came from thinking about Joe's future. That would be a lie. Instead, what gave her pause were the addled words of a child.

"You're trying to make her mental." The wrenching in Foxy's gut ceased, and an eerie calm settled. A calm that felt right. "She said you were trying to make her mental."

"Thank you for stopping by Commissioner Benson but—"

Rich didn't get a chance to excuse the commissioner because Foxy went on.

"You're trying to diagnose Daria with a mental illness." The flash of acid roiled in Foxy's belly. It left behind the taste of metal, like the copper of a penny, in her mouth. "Money? You're doing this because of money?"

Once again, Rich tried to come between the two, perhaps to smooth the waters. But these waters were shark-invested, and Foxy had caught big game on the hook.

"If you want your fiancé to prosper," said

Commissioner Benson. "If you want your certification rubber-stamped, then you'll play along."

Foxy shook her head, a warm glow of certainty radiating from her entire being. "Whatever you're doing, Joe would never play along with this."

"Excuse me." Joe's voice was amplified throughout the room. He stood on stage at a microphone stand. Standing by his side was Charlotte O'Dell. "I dreamed of this day since I was a child."

A hush fell over the room as they all waited for Joe Matthews to accept the honor that had been bestowed upon him. Foxy had the urge to run to the stage and yank him away from the dangerous pool he was about to wade into. Something in her gut told her she didn't have to.

"Ever since I was put in the system as a foster kid," Joe continued, "I knew that I wanted to help those who felt powerless. The best way to do that was through the law. Or so I thought. I've always prized logic over feelings, facts over emotion. This time I'm choosing feelings and emotion."

Joe's gaze found Foxy in the crowd before he continued. And when he did, Foxy knew with certainty that everything between them for now and in the future would be just fine. She didn't feel it in her gut. She knew it in her heart.

CHAPTER TWENTY-ONE

oe's toe bumped against the riser at the podium. The jolt sent a screech of feedback through the microphone. Inside his body, he felt his gut, his heart, his head shake with turbulence. He had a moment of doubt where he wondered if he was truly prepared for this new turn his life was taking.

Searching the crowd, he found a beacon when he saw Foxy. He caught sight of her where he'd left her, standing with Rich. She wasn't smiling. She looked very concerned. Her gaze followed Commissioner Benson as he walked off.

Joe wanted to leap down off the stage and go to her. To go to Benson and deck the commissioner for what he might have said to upset Foxy. But Joe knew he didn't need to. He could see it in her narrowed gaze. Foxy had already made the man out to be the villain without any need for the awful facts that Joe had collected. Because Foxy trusted her gut, she saw things clearly. Where he needed facts and figures.

When her gaze found his, she didn't smile. She still looked concerned. Did she doubt him? Did she think he would take this job after learning the facts? Well, if she did, Joe was about to make his stance on the matter crystal clear.

He turned his attention back to the microphone, took a deep breath, and took that hard left turn that would change his life's trajectory forever.

"I dreamed of this day since I was a child," he began. A hush fell over the room as they all waited for him to accept the honor that had been bestowed upon him. "Ever since I was put in the system as a foster kid, I knew that I wanted to help those who felt powerless. The best way to do that was through the law. Or so I thought. I've always prized logic over feelings, facts over emotion. This time I'm choosing feelings and emotion."

A restless rustle went through the crowd as they tried to gauge where this speech was going. The only person's opinion Joe cared about was Foxy's. When he found her again, a beatific smile crossed her face. A smile that said *I know you. I'm with you. I love you.*

Joe nearly forgot what he was about to say in the prepared speech. All he wanted was to kiss that smile on Foxy's face. Not yet, but soon. After he took the first step on the long path of the work he chose to do.

"I will not be accepting the appointment as county District Attorney. I will be going into private practice." Joe motioned Charlotte to his side. "With the help of Charlotte O'Dell as my partner, we'll be launching a lawsuit to stop the taking of foster children's survivor benefits, veteran's benefits, and Social Security benefits by the county and state."

A gasp went up through the crowd. Joe ignored what his ears heard and only focused on what his eyes saw. His Foxy didn't look surprised at all. Of course she didn't. Because she knew.

"Just as my family and my friends, and the love of my life stood by me, I hope you all will support me in this crusade to do the right thing for the most vulnerable amongst us; the children who have no parents to turn to."

There were a few seconds of stunned silence. Followed by raucous applause. Joe clasped Charlotte's hand in his and thrust their arms into the air.

The crowd swarmed the stage. Joe moved through quickly as possible, his eyes on Foxy as she stood still, waiting for him. There were many claps on his back. Many hands reaching out to shake his.

When Joe reached Foxy, he reached for her hands. They were warm and familiar. He brought them to his lips and kissed each of her fingers before finally placing his lips upon hers.

"Why didn't you tell me?" she said.

"It honestly didn't occur to me that you didn't already know," he said. "You told me you felt something was wrong."

"You listened to me."

"But I didn't believe. I won't make that mistake again."

Foxy wrapped her arms around his neck. "I had a feeling it would all work out between us."

Joe pulled her in closer until there wasn't a breath of space between them. "Well, this was the only logical conclusion to our story."

He bent his head to her and captured her lips. Their kiss ignited a fire inside him. The blaze burned so brightly Joe had a moment's fear that everyone in the vicinity might be burned by how much he loved this woman. That fear quickly died as the embers grew. The love he and Foxy shared was now and would continue to be a force for good.

EPILOGUE

The chime let off a high-pitched shrill, breaking up the sounds of the music coming from the stage. A few listeners turned to glare at Will Matthews. He shrugged unapologetically. It wasn't as if his ringing phone during the performance had made things any worse.

The drummer was a beat behind the keyboardist. The guitarist's E-string was out of tune. The vocalist had mixed up the words of the popular song that they were butchering.

Will was sure his ringing phone couldn't possibly make the cacophony of sounds any worse. Still, he put silenced the device. Though he knew that wouldn't stop the person on the other end of the phone from reaching out to him.

He was right.

Barely a second later and the phone was vibrating on the dining table. The light from the face of the phone flashed an alert in case the bumping and jumping around of the device weren't enough. Again, the guests at the table next to him sent him a glare.

Instead of a shrug, Will sent the man a glare right back. It was clear the man was a lightweight because after only three seconds into the stare-off, the other man dropped his gaze. As if the man stood a chance against a Matthews. Including this one.

Will had stood tall, with his chest puffed up while he disappointed the man who meant the most to him in this world. When Will had broken the news to his adoptive father that had broken the old man's heart, Will hadn't blinked. Haran Matthews had taught him better than that. But Will's mind had been made up that day, and though he knew his father would never be as proud of him as he was of his other son's, Will had down what was best for himself.

He had no excuse why he was now in a dive bar listening to the butchering of old songs made into something unrecognizable by today's rebel youth. The last act had taken an old Beatles song and made it sound like frogs croaking to their death. The current act was thankfully finishing up a poor man's rendition of an Ella Fitzgerald song that made Will certain he was dreaming a little nightmare.

As that band cleared off, Will's phone took another opportunity to vibrate and flash once more. He knew this would continue until he answered. Now that Joe was out of the military, his brother would dog him until Will answered.

"Shouldn't you be in court or something?" was Will's greeting to his older brother.

"No, because I'll be headed to church instead."

"Not surprising being the kid of a preacher."

"She said yes."

Will paused to stare down at his phone. On the face of the receiver was his brother's name and number. He placed the device back to his ear.

"You finally told Foxy how you feel?"

"I did."

"And now you're getting married?"

"We are."

"Bro that's the best news I've heard in a long time."

Will was truly happy for Joe. He was the most serious brother of the Matthews clan, but he'd been head over heels in love with Foxy James for as long as Will could remember. Their brother Charlie had been in love with Savy James for just as long. What was it about those James sisters that stole a Matthews boy's attention?

"Sav and Fox want a double wedding," Joe was saying. "We'll need you home."

"Yeah… yeah."

Will wasn't sure if his brother could hear the lack of enthusiasm in his voice. He'd made his visits back to the Flying Cross Ranch fewer and far between after he'd disappointed their father with his choices in life. The pang in his heart was still a real thing. Though when he saw the next act walk out onto the stage, his heartbeats picked up a few beats.

"There's so much to do, and we're going to need you," Joe was saying.

"Yeah… right."

The sultry songstress wrapped a slender hand around the microphone. Every man in the room leaned forward as her vibrant red lips came close mic. Will included. But he'd always leaned forward whenever she parted those lips in song, or just to say hello.

"You never know," said Joe. "By the time you get here, there might be three weddings. I wouldn't be surprised if Topher finds Tricksy and proposes."

That brought Will out of his stupor. He blinked once, twice. But his vision was still filled with the songbird on stage. She opened her mouth and the sweetest sounds began to fill the room.

"Hey, is that Tricksy I hear-"

"Joe, I gotta go. I'll talk to you soon."

Will hit disconnect before his brother could ask any more questions, or hear any more incriminating evidence. Namely the fact that Will was seated at the back of a dive bar, in the shadows, listening to his brother's ex as she crooned a somebody-done-somebody-wrong love song. Because if his father, or his brothers, knew of his latest life-altering decision, it would definitely be a long time before they saw hide or hair of him again.

You may think you've guessed Will's secret.
But his secret crush on his brother's ex is just the beginning.
Find out the rest in *His Vow to Adore,*
Book Three in the Flying Cross Ranch Romances!

Shanae Johnson was raised by Saturday Morning cartoons and After School Specials. She still doesn't understand why there isn't a life lesson that ties the issues of the day together just before bedtime. While she's still waiting for the meaning of it all, she writes stories to try and figure it all out. Her books are wholesome and sweet, but her are heroes are hot and heroines are full of sass!

And by the way, the E elongates the A. So it's pronounced Shan-aaaaaaaa. Perfect for a hero to call out across the moors, or up to a balcony, or to blare outside her window on a boombox. If you hear him calling her name, please send him her way!

You can sign up for Shanae's Reader Group and receive a FREE NOVELLA in this world at

http://bit.ly/ShanaeJohnsonReaders

Also By Shanae Johnson

a Flying Cross Ranch Romance

His Vow to Love

His Vow to Treasure

His Vow to Adore

His Vow to Trust

His Vow to Respect

His Vow to Defend

The Silver Star Ranch Romances

His Pledge to Honor

His Pledge to Cherish

His Pledge to Protect

His Pledge to Obey

His Pledge to Have

His Pledge to Hold

The Rangers of Purple Heart

The Rancher takes his Convenient Bride

The Rancher takes his Best Friend's Sister

The Rancher takes his Runaway Bride

The Rancher takes his Star Crossed Love

The Rancher takes his Love at First Sight

The Rancher takes his Last Chance at Love

The Brides of Purple Heart

On His Bended Knee

Hand Over His Heart

Offering His Arm

His Permanent Scar

Having His Back

In Over His Head

Always On His Mind

Every Step He Takes

In His Good Hands

Light Up His Life

Strength to Stand

The Rebel Royals series

The King and the Kindergarten Teacher

The Prince and the Pie Maker

The Duke and the DJ

The Marquis and the Magician's Assistant

The Princess and the Principal

www.ingramcontent.com/pod-product-compliance
Lightning Source LLC
Chambersburg PA
CBHW050342160726
48002CB00001B/424